SHARON E. McKAY

ENEMY TERRITORY

annick press
toronto + new york + vancouver

© 2012 Sharon E. McKay
Edited by Barbara Berson
Copyedited by Catherine Marjoribanks
Maps by Tina Holdcroft
Cover and interior design by Kong Njo

Annick Press Ltd.

We acknowledge the support of the Canada Council for the Arts, the Ontario
Arts Council, and the Government of Canada through the Canada Book Fund
(CBF) for our publishing activities.

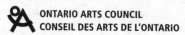

ONTARIO ARTS COUNCIL
CONSEIL DES ARTS DE L'ONTARIO

Text from *I Shall Not Hate: A Gaza Doctor's Journey on the Road to Peace and Human
Dignity* © Izzeldin Abuelaish 2010, is reprinted with the permission of the author;
of Bloomsbury Publishing Plc; and of Random House of Canada

Cover photos: Jerusalem, an alley in the Jewish quarter © iStockphoto.com/
gil yarom; young boys © iStockphoto.com/Andrew Penner

Attempts have been made to locate copyright holders of quoted material.
Please contact the publisher with any concerns.

Cataloging in Publication

McKay, Sharon E

     Enemy territory / Sharon E. McKay.

ISBN 978-1-55451-431-1 (bound).—ISBN 978-1-55451-430-4 (pbk.)

     1. Arab-Israeli conflict—Juvenile fiction. I. Title.

PS8575.K2898E64 2012   jC813'.6   C2012-902111-3

Distributed in Canada by:
Firefly Books Ltd.
66 Leek Crescent
Richmond Hill, ON
L4B 1H1

Published in the U.S.A. by:
Annick Press (U.S.) Ltd.
Distributed in the U.S.A. by:
Firefly Books (U.S.) Inc.
P.O. Box 1338, Ellicott Station
Buffalo, NY 14205

Printed in Canada

Visit us at: www.annickpress.com
Visit Sharon E. McKay at: www.sharonmckay.ca

Every story is informed by something: a thought, an image, or a character, perhaps. In this case it was a single sentiment expressed by my cousin, who lives in Belfast, Northern Ireland.

We are tired. We want peace.

—Detective Inspector William Daniel,
Royal Ulster Constabulary (Retired),
Member of the Order of the British Empire (MBE)

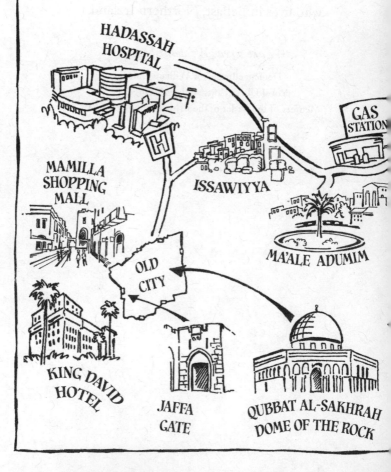

JERUSALEM
AND SURROUNDING AREA

HADASSAH HOSPITAL

GAS STATION

MAMILLA SHOPPING MALL

ISSAWIYYA

MA'ALE ADUMIM

OLD CITY

KING DAVID HOTEL

JAFFA GATE

QUBBAT AL-SAKHRAH
DOME OF THE ROCK

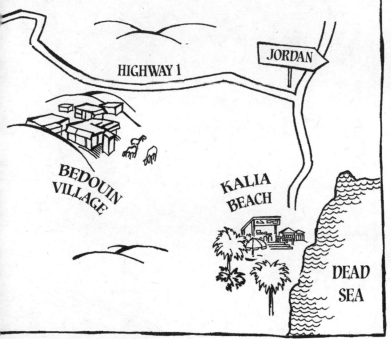

Prologue

This is the story of Sam and Yusuf. Sam is Jewish and an Israeli. Yusuf is Muslim and a Palestinian. Both were born into war. Two horrific events would change their world forever.

Yusuf
Beit Lahm (Bethlehem), West Bank

Yusuf steps out of the house and races across the small courtyard. Mama's pigeons flap their wings furiously against the wooden bars of their cages as his shoes slap against the packed earth.

Ducking under an olive tree that curls around the door, Yusuf yanks the iron knob and steps into the road. Noisy goats trot toward him, kicking up swirls of fine yellow sand, and the dusty goatherd follows behind, keeping some sort of order by wielding his long crook.

Yusuf spots his father walking farther down the road and raises his hand in greeting. But Baba's eyes are cast down, his face creased by worry and too much sunshine. On most days

Baba wears Western-style trousers and a white shirt, but today his head is wrapped in a *keffiyeh*. His streaked gray beard is cropped shorter than those of most Palestinian men, and his white shirt and baggy pants balloon out as he walks.

"Baba!" Yusuf calls.

Baba waves back, and before long he is standing in front of his son. "Look how tall you are, Yusuf. Soon I will be looking up into your eyes. Where are you going?"

"Mama wants me to find Nasser and bring him home," Yusuf replies, half hoping that Baba will say, "No. Walk with me instead." But his father's face darkens at the sound of his firstborn son's name. His parents worry a lot about Nasser, about the trouble he gets into.

"Go and get your brother." Baba waves Yusuf on. "And tie your shoes." Now Baba smiles—a rare sight. Yusuf would never tie his shoes again if it meant that his father would keep smiling.

Yusuf knows where to look for Nasser. With the laces on his running shoes tied tight, he runs down narrow, crowded streets, up onto wooden walkways, through laneways, across open sewers and muck patches before coming to Manger Square in the middle of Beit Lahm.

As usual, sweaty tourists are swigging water from plastic bottles as they perch on a wall near the little door that leads into the Christian church. The Christians call his city

Bethlehem, the place where their Savior, Jesus, was born. But Jesus was a Jew, Yusuf thinks, so why do the Christians call themselves Christians instead of Jews? It's confusing. Baba explained it once but it didn't help.

Yusuf races across the open square paved with polished stones, past the flagpoles, the falafel seller, and a café serving carrot, fig, and pomegranate juice. The sweet smell of bread and pastries wafts from a restaurant. But when Yusuf makes a sharp turn up the road the streets become steep and narrow. Laundry lines are slung across alleyways, over twisted TV antennas, satellite dishes, shade canopies, and slack black wires strung from house to house.

"Hey, Yusuf!"

At the top of Frères Street, Yusuf turns to see Mazen and Yasser running toward him, their silhouettes blurred against the noonday sun. Lately Yusuf has been having trouble seeing things clearly. His mother gave him his uncle's thick, black-rimmed glasses, but when he tried them on, his older sister, Mira, said that he looked like a giant bug. Now he'd rather be blind than wear them.

"Yusuf, here!" Mazen stops and pulls back his leg, and a great, whirling, fuzzy orb comes hurtling toward Yusuf. He stops it with his foot—it's a new, scuff-free American soccer ball.

When he kicks it back it sails over his friends' heads. "Yes! Call me Salem, the best Palestinian soccer player of all time!" Yusuf does a victory dance. "Where did you get the ball?"

"My cousin in America." Mazen beams with pride.

Now Yasser is motioning to the others—he has something he wants to show them. He pulls a potato out of his pocket and holds it up in the air.

"How about we stuff this in the tailpipe of Abu Azam's car?"

All three gaze across the street to a café, where Abu Azam is sitting on a spindly chair in front of a gently turning fan. He is sipping carrot juice, sucking on a water pipe, and rolling dice, all at the same time. His patched-up car—part Toyota, part Honda, with a bunch of Russian parts thrown in—is parked on a hill nearby.

Yusuf and Mazen nod in unison. No one deserves a potato shoved up his pipe more than Abu Azam. He's mean. He'll give a kid a smack, twist his ear, even kick him in the pants. And for what? For nothing!

"Come on." Mazen grabs the potato out of Yasser's hand and leads the way, with Yasser and Yusuf hot on his heels.

Crouching behind a pile of bricks, Yusuf and Yasser watch as Mazen ducks, zigzags, and weaves until he reaches the car. When he glances back over his shoulder, Yasser and Yusuf give him the all-clear signal. Then Mazen rams the potato into the tailpipe and gives it a swift smack with a flat palm. He scurries back to the others like a crab on a beach.

"How do we get him to start the car?" whispers Yusuf.

"He has to be getting hungry—it's past time for *ghada*. He'll leave soon, be patient," Yasser hisses. By the look of Abu Azam's belly he seldom misses the main meal of the day.

Sure enough, Abu Azam bids good day to the men in the café, slowly walks over to his car, and gets in.

"Wait, look!" Yasser points to an Israeli military convoy roaring toward them through the dust—four armored vehicles in a line. Soldiers, some pointing guns, peer out from the vehicles. They are clearly on high alert.

"Yusuf, look! There's your brother." Mazen nudges him.

Yusuf looks directly across the street, and there is Nasser, standing on a wooden walkway, transfixed. What's he looking at? What's that in his hand?

Now the convoy is bearing down. Yusuf looks back at his brother. Is he holding a rock? Nasser steps off the walkway and is now at the edge of the road.

"Nasser!" Yusuf leaps up. Cars, bikes, and trucks veer off the path of the oncoming convoy. Abu Azam puts his keys in the ignition. The convoy is almost upon them.

"Nasser, you will get in trouble. Think about Mama. Think about Baba," Yusuf whispers under his breath.

The convoy is directly in front of him. Nasser lifts his arm and takes aim. Yusuf screams, "*Nasser, no!*"

Yusuf doesn't see it coming. How could he? A sharp bang. Is it a gunshot? The pain is searing. One moment he is reeling backward and the next he is on fire. "*Yusuf!*" he hears Mazen scream. And then, nothing.

Sam
Jerusalem

Sam tosses his knapsack on a chair and thumps down at the kitchen table. Judy, his sister, doesn't even look up. Today, like most days, his breakfast consists of a cucuber and tomato salad, two hard-boiled eggs, white cheese, and olives.

Grasping a damp cloth, Sam's mother, his Ima, bustles around trying to clean up but only manages to launch crumbs in all directions. Ima is a twelfth-generation Jerusalemite. Ima's family lived on this land before Moses, that's what Great-Aunt Esther said, and no one argued with her. What was the point? The way Great-Aunt Esther told the story, with gusts of garlic and flailing arms, their relatives floated down the Nile in reed baskets ahead of Moses. Never mind that it made no sense.

His father, Abba, is fiddling with the radio dials. Sam is convinced that it's the oldest radio in Israel—*Abraham* owned it. Sam bites into a hard-boiled egg. The yoke sticks to his front teeth.

"Let's see if we still exist." Abba tunes the radio to 93.9. The announcer mentions something about the football team and a new stadium. "Footballers! That bunch of prima donnas do not need a new stadium. Better they should win the World Cup. Ha! Ramat Gan Stadium is good enough for them." Abba switches to Galei Tzahal, the military station. There is something on the news about the settlers. "Those religious settlers are as much a threat as the Arabs," Abba grumbles. Sam chases an olive around his plate. There is a repeat of the prime minister's speech, something about "the enemies' cult of death" and "we too are entitled . . ." Then comes a beep. "We interrupt this program . . ." There has been an ambush near Kiryat Arba in the West Bank. Four Israelis have been killed. Hamas is claiming responsibility for the attack.

Sam pushes away his plate. Everyone, even Abba, falls silent for a moment. And then everything goes back to near-normal. There is no such thing as normal-normal here.

"Samuel, take a sweater. And don't forget your piano lesson after school." Ima folds the dishcloth and places it over the tap.

"*Beseder*, it's all good," mumbles Sam as he looks through the painted iron bars that protect the kitchen window. There are bars on all their windows. It is the same in every Israeli house. "*Yalla bye*," he calls out to her.

"Be careful. Take your mobile phone and call me when you get to school," his mother calls after him. Ima worries all the time. Sam grabs his phone, which he calls a "pelly," and heads down the hall toward the front door.

When Sam leaves his apartment building the door bangs behind him and locks automatically. Their housing complex was built with pale pink Jerusalem stone. The stones give a message to the world: *We are as permanent as the pyramids. We are here forever.* Sam adjusts his knapsack, ducks under the fig tree his mother planted when he was born, unlocks the outside gate, and hops down a few steps. The gate shuts and locks behind him.

The neighbor's huge dog lets out a deep, threatening growl. Sam barks back and takes the last four steps in one leap.

Mr. Rosenthal, the neighbor, is taking his clippers to the branches of an olive tree. Mr. Rosenthal has a daughter, named Hannah, who got married and moved away. Sam used to wave to her but she never waved back. Hannah's husband was a widower with four children when they got married, and then they had another six children together. Hannah's husband studies the Torah all day. Hannah and her father fight a lot. One day everyone heard him hollering, "The only thing that husband of yours brought to the marriage was his hemorrhoids from sitting on his ass all day long. He is *ohley hinam*, a freeloader." Mr. Rosenthal doesn't think Hannah and her family should be living where they are, in a place called Ma'ale Adumim. He calls it a settlement on Palestinian land, and Israelis do not belong there. She says it's a suburb of Jerusalem.

Once he's far enough away, Sam holds up a clenched fist, furrows his brow, and repeats, "What you are doing is wrong for Israel!" He does a great imitation of Mr. Rosenthal.

How can Sam get out of piano lessons? He wants to quit, but Ima says, "Nonsense. If Jews had been quitters we would not have survived five thousand years." Ima always makes it sound as though quitting piano lessons would be letting down the Jewish people from the beginning of time!

Sam walks down the laneway toward a busy street. That's when he spots Annah Weise, another neighbor, walking her scabby dog. She is always asking him personal questions. He ducks behind a garden wall and waits until she turns the corner. When he's sure she's gone, he comes back to the sidewalk and looks around. Where's Ari? They meet at this corner every morning.

"Sam, over here!" Ari waves to him from across the street. He's holding something in the air. Is that a new soccer ball? "Hurry up," yells Ari. He bounces the ball from knee to knee.

Sam raises his hand in greeting and turns his head from left to right. He looks but does not see. He laughs and runs. A military truck hurtles around the corner. Sam steps into its path.

CHAPTER 1

❖

Hadassah Hospital, West Jerusalem

Sam maneuvered his crutches around a collection of ladders, paint cans, yards of plastic sheeting, and fold-up DANGER signs. Hadassah Hospital was always under construction, although a better word might have been *destruction*. There were always repair people tearing something up. He had been to the Ein Kerem campus of Hadassah Hospital for his operation. Mount Scopus was smaller, nicer, and, even with the destruction, quieter.

Sam carried on down the hall, passed the nursing station, took a left, and cruised toward the elevator. He was using hospital crutches made of ultra-lightweight aluminum. The rubber padding on the armrests was already making his armpits sore. A padded shoe, clasped together with Velcro, surrounded his right foot and lower leg. It wasn't a cast, just protection from accidental knocks. He punched the "Down" button. *Come on, come on.* Sam willed the elevator door to open.

"Where are you going?" The voice was stern, loud, and raspy. *Damn.* Sam shook his head. "You must not leave the floor. Dinner is in one hour."

Hopping on his good foot, Sam swiveled on the crutches and looked directly into a large, flat face edged with fuzzy red hair that sprang out in coils like, what's-her-name, that Greek goddess with the snake hair. Worse, her eyebrows resembled two upturned crow's wings glued, or maybe nailed, to her forehead. A name tag as big as a street sign hovered above bulging breasts. The tag read, "Luba." In English it rhymed with tuba. She kind of looked like a tuba.

"I'm going to meet my mother in the lobby." There, he'd told a barefaced lie. Now, what was Tuba-Luba going to do about it?

"One hour, you be back." Tuba-Luba was Russian. She spoke Hebrew as if she had a ball of spit collected at the back of her throat. She turned and stormed away.

The elevator door slid open. Stepping inside, Sam scowled as he pushed "Lobby." The doors closed and the elevator descended.

When the doors opened on the lobby, an orderly standing behind a wheelchair motioned with his head for

Sam to get off. Sam stepped aside as the orderly spun the wheelchair around and backed into the elevator. The kid in the chair gazed up at Sam. One eye was piercing; the other was covered by a black eye-patch. The boys' eyes locked. The kid looked about the same age as Sam—fourteen, probably tall, olive-colored skin, shaggy black hair, shoulders pinned to his ears. Sam peered at the kid's feet—cheap running shoes. Safe bet he was a Palestinian, likely Muslim, not Christian. Great, an Arab pirate was in the building. With a faint roll and a swish, the elevator doors closed and Pirate Boy disappeared.

Sam swung the crutches forward. His upper-body strength had improved substantially since his accident two months ago. He caught his reflection in a window. From the waist up he thought he might even pass for "hunky," like an actor in an American television show. Below the waist, his legs—well, that was another matter.

"Sam, over here."

Alina was leaning against a chair at the far end of the lobby. She was hard to miss. Her metallic-blue hair, straight and cut with bangs like Cleopatra's, shimmered under the harsh fluorescent lights. She was beautiful, in a Natalie Portman sort of way. And it didn't matter if she was bald under that wig, either.

"Hi." Not for the first time, Sam wished he had a better opening line.

"You took forever." Alina smiled.

Sam blushed for no particular reason. Alina wasn't his girlfriend or anything. If they both hadn't been stuck in the hospital they likely wouldn't even have known each other. Why would a hotshot, almost-pro tennis player, with or without cancer, talk to a kid who might have to have his leg chopped off?

"I was under *nurse* interrogation," said Sam.

Alina nodded. She had been in and out of the hospital for over a year. No further explanation was needed. She understood.

"I'll text you next time I'm late. I get my new pelly tonight," said Sam. Technically, mobile phones were not allowed in the hospital, but no one enforced that rule.

"Mine's new too." Alina pulled a shiny phone out of her pocket and waved it around. "And I've programmed your number into it. Do you want to go to the PR or the cafeteria?"

"PR," said Sam.

"Right, lead the way," replied Alina as she stood up and led the way.

She pushed a medical pole ahead of her. A bag of clear liquid was attached to a slack, thin tube that led from the bag to her arm. Sam had never seen her without the pole and bag of liquid meds.

"Must be a quiet day," said Alina when they reached the threshold of the empty room.

"PR" stood for playroom—but what fourteen-year-old would admit to going to a playroom? It was just down the hall beside the emergency rooms. A bank of computers lined one wall, and coloring tables, complete with plastic cups filled with crayons, were strung along another wall. Leatherette sofas and oversized chairs were scattered throughout, and in the middle, as ridiculous as it seemed to both of them, was a fake spacecraft, a cone-shaped capsule decorated with demonic-looking blond children dancing in a meadow. It was a bomb shelter built in 1948, the year the state of Israel was declared. The shelter seated ten. Sam pursed his lips and thought that kid number eleven was out of luck. A plaque nailed to it said that the hospital had been built around the shelter. Totally ridiculous.

Alina eased herself down into a chair. Extending his injured right leg, Sam lowered himself onto the sofa. The sofa made an embarrassing farty sound.

"How's your leg?" asked Alina.

"It's still attached." Sam tried to sound cavalier, like losing a leg was an everyday sort of thing, like losing an umbrella. But what did he have to complain about? Alina could lose her life. Sometimes, though, he thought he'd rather die then let them take his leg off.

"Do you remember anything about your accident yet?"

When other people asked him the same question he got ticked off, but when Alina asked him it felt like she cared.

"I remember eating breakfast. My father was listening to the radio. There was an attack, a bombing somewhere. My father always gets really upset. He doesn't show it, he doesn't even say anything. His sister was murdered in a suicide bombing."

"I'm sorry," Alina murmured.

Sam shrugged. What was there to say? Many people had lost someone in attacks, or during the intifadas, when Palestinians attacked the Israelis who were living in the West Bank, the Gaza Strip, and Israel too. Besides, it was a long time ago. "She was twenty-five years old. She used to read me stories. My favorite was *Dira Lehaskir—An Apartment for Rent*."

Alina clapped her hands. "'And thus, in a beautiful valley, among vineyards and fields, stands a tower of five floors. And in the tower, to this day, live all the good neighbors together, happily and peacefully.' My *savta*, grandmother, read it to me all the time."

"My aunt told jokes too, but only in English. She went to university in New York. She said that if I wanted to go to school in America I had to improve my English. I remember a joke she used to tell. Ready?" asked Sam.

Alina nodded.

"Knock, knock."

"Who's there?" Alina giggled.

"Sascha." Sam furrowed his brow.

"Sascha who?" asked Alina.

"Sascha lot of questions you have!" Sam bumped his gums like an old man. Alina grimaced. "It was funnier when I was seven years old. My aunt was the only person in my family who told jokes." Sam stopped. That was the first joke he could remember telling in years and years, maybe since his aunt had been killed.

"Then what did you do?" Alina pressed on. "You know, the day it happened."

"I left for school. I passed Mr. Rosenthal's house. He's really nice, but he and his daughter argue all the time, especially since she married this seriously religious guy and moved away." Sam mimicked Mr. Rosenthal, all sputter and bluster: "'Listen to me, these *settlements* are wrong. Think of your children. Think of Israel. We need peace.'" Sam wrung his hands and then, palms out, he pleaded.

Alina giggled, then went all serious all of a sudden. "But you want peace too, right? I mean, it's what we all want."

"Yeah, but it's a two-way street," Sam said, and then thought, *What a weird thing to say*.

"Sorry, go back to your story." Alina looked intense.

"I remember hiding from Annah Weise. She's a nosy neighbor. She carries around this ugly, scabby dog like it's a bracelet. She used to carry it in a purse but it kept pissing on her stuff. Now it pisses on her arm."

Alina laughed. Sam thought that her laugh was the best sound ever.

"After that, I walked out into the street. Ari was on the other side. He was waving, or maybe yelling. I can't remember anything after that. And Ari doesn't come to the hospital much. I think the place gives him the creeps." Both grew silent. Since her diagnosis, Alina had lost friends too.

Alina's smile disappeared and she lowered her voice. "Remember when we first met? It was in the day clinic, remember?"

Sam nodded. How could he forget? Her hair had been brown then, streaked with gold, and tied back in a ponytail. He'd been so amazed that she would even speak to him that he could hardly say a word in return. He'd recognized her from her pictures in the newspaper—she was the Next Big Thing. She was going to take the tennis world by storm, put Israel on the world tennis map.

"I heard the nurses talking in the clinic. They said that after your accident you were dead for three minutes. Do you remember dying?" Wide-eyed, her voice hushed, Alina leaned in to hear Sam's answer.

"I don't remember anything." He looked directly into Alina's eyes. They were the color of the sky on a perfect day. And then he understood. How could he be so dense? He had died, and Alina was dying. He shook his head.

"There was nothing?" she asked again.

Should he make something up? What did they say about dying? Something about a white light? "We have to get back to our rooms for dinner," he said sadly. Really, he couldn't think of a thing to say or a way to help.

Alina struggled to stand. There were tears in her eyes. She walked out of the PR and turned toward the far elevators. Sam followed.

"What are you doing after dinner? We could have a coffee."

"I'll text you, promise." She turned back, smiled, and walked away.

Sam watched her go. It was hard to tell which was skinnier, Alina or that pole she was pushing around.

Sam took the elevator to his floor and cruised down the hall. He passed the nursing station, took a right, hopped around the DANGER sign and all the crap on the floor, and, balancing on his crutches, gave the door to his room a push. The door banged open, and Sam looked directly into the one good eye of Pirate Boy.

CHAPTER 2

❖

Who Is My Roommate?

Tuba-Luba came up from behind Sam as he stood on the threshold of his hospital room—a sneak attack. "Good, you are back." She spread a bear-paw-sized hand across Sam's back and gave him a little shove. Sam scowled.

The room was small, painted light blue, with two lockers against one wall and a curtain that separated the two beds. Sam's bed was beside the window. Pirate Boy, next to the door, was lying under the hospital's sheets, which were all imprinted with the Star of David.

"*Fee 'endakum ghurfa*," Tuba-Luba said. Pirate Boy gave the nurse a pained smile. Sam rolled his eyes—he didn't know what it meant, but her Arabic didn't sound any better than her Hebrew. "Sam, get into your *peejama* and say hello to Yusuf." It sounded like a command, not an introduction.

Sam nodded but didn't open his mouth. Likely Pirate Boy did not speak Hebrew. "Yusuf, say hello to Sam."

Yusuf tilted his head and focused with his right eye. He could see clearly if there was enough light. This kid looked about fourteen years old, Yusuf's age. He had light brown hair, light skin, a square head, and a matching square chin. The nurse was speaking to him in Hebrew, so he had to be Israeli.

Luba pulled the curtain. It stuck midway. She gave it a yank, cursed at it in Russian, and the room was instantly divided in two. The curtain was gray-blue and, from Sam's point of view, as good as a wall.

Yusuf watched the shadows behind the curtain move around. Luba was helping the Israeli kid get into bed. She took off his large padded boot and put it into the locker. What was wrong with his foot? Or was it his leg?

"Samuel, Yusuf has been at the Ein Kerem hospital too. He speaks Arabic and perfect Hebrew. Maybe you two have met?" Luba's gravelly voice pitched into soprano as she batted back the curtain. Yusuf looked over at the Israeli kid, who was now in bed. He didn't look happy.

Sam looked at Pirate Boy. It was unlikely that the boy spoke perfect Hebrew, and they had most definitely not met.

"Let me see your leg," said Tuba-Luba. Without so much as an *excuse me*, and in full view of this new Arab roommate, Tuba-Luba tossed back Sam's sheets, peered down, and sniffed.

Sam yanked the sheet back over his foot. "Go away!" Did she think he had gangrene? Sam hated her, but not because she stank of French cigarettes and sickly sweet French soap. And not because she was Russian, either, although he'd overheard plenty of Israelis talk about Russian Jews as though they were either snobs who were ruining the country or lowlifes who were up to no good. No, Sam hated Tuba-Luba because she was bossy, because she never listened, because she treated him like a child, and because he'd overheard her telling another nurse that Israelis had no culture. Ha! They had plenty of culture, whatever that meant. Anyway, he hated her.

"Your leg—is there pain?" Tuba-Luba tossed the sheet aside again, picked up Sam's sore leg, and massaged his calf.

Sam winced with pain but he would not give her the satisfaction of admitting it. His ankle was the size of an orange. The last time the infection was this bad they'd talked about transplanting bone from one leg to the other. His fever wasn't too high, though. Tomorrow he would have an MRI and more X-rays, and then he would be given some new wonder drugs. He had heard it all before. The main thing was that he could still feel his leg and his toes, which really meant he could still feel the pain.

Yusuf kept glancing over at the Israeli. Yusuf had been

in the hospital for two months and in that entire time he'd made one friend, an American kid named Art who'd broken his leg at some camp. Art had taught him two things: first, Israelis (and Americans) knew next to nothing about Palestinians, and second, how to pronounce "p." There is no "p" sound in Arabic. Art liked to demonstrate. "Keep trying—*pisssssssssssss*. Make a popping sound. Now pull back your mouth, like this." Art repeated it with accompanying spit. They practiced for hours. "And if you don't like what someone is saying, tell them to 'shut up.'" Art demonstrated that too. Then one day Art's mother arrived from New York, packed his bag, and that was that. Still, Yusuf kept practicing his "p"s.

"Do not get up without ringing for the nurse." Using her hands like hatchets, Tuba-Luba tucked the sheets around Sam. Then she adjusted the blinds, and finally she turned around like a battleship about to parallel park. "Yusuf, your prosthetic eye will be examined tomorrow morning. Now you too must be a good boy and rest." Luba gave them both the evil eye, then spun away on her rubber heels.

Sam's ears perked up. Did she say prosthetic eye? Did that mean the other boy had one, or was he getting one? Either way, Pirate Boy had a hole in his head.

"Merkava," Yusuf muttered under his breath.

Tuba-Luba either did not hear or ignored him. She left the room without a backward glance. And did the Pirate just say "Merkava"? As in the name of an Israeli army tank? Maybe there was hope for the guy.

Sam gazed over at his roommate. The Arab pirate-kid lay in the bed like a dead fish. An Arab was not exactly friendship material, but Sam was short on friends. There was Alina, of course, but she was getting sicker every day. All the pink balloons and stuff weren't going to change her diagnosis. And why did people think that a cancer patient liked pink balloons anyway?

"Why are you here?" asked Sam (standard opening question).

"Tests." Yusuf shrugged (standard reply).

Sam chewed his bottom lip while considering Pirate Boy's one-word response. Fine, if he didn't want to be friends they could be enemies. "What are they looking for, brain cells?" Great retort. Sam congratulated himself.

"I have an eye infection," Yusuf snapped back.

"Which eye has the infection? The one that's missing or the one that's blind?" Sam grinned, except it was more of a smirk.

Yusuf pulled up the blanket. "Leave me alone."

"You speak Hebrew, but you're an Arab, right?" asked Sam. This was curious. How could Arabs learn any language if they all went to super-religious Muslim schools that taught Rock Throwing 101 or How Great Is Jihad?

Yusuf ignored him.

"Say 'pirate.'" Sam, speaking in English, leaned across the gulf between the two hospital beds.

Yusuf shook his head.

"Ha! You can't pronounce 'p.'"

"Piss off," Yusuf shot back.

Sam's eyebrows shot up. That was impressive. "Do you speak English?"

Yusuf shrugged. Let the Israeli think what he wanted. Yusuf didn't know much English, but his father spoke it, as well as Arabic and Hebrew. There weren't a lot of Palestinians Yusuf's age who spoke Hebrew. His friends laughed at him for wasting his time learning it, especially his brother, Nasser. He said, "The language of the Jews is like dirt in my mouth." But Baba said, "One day everyone will grow tired of fighting, and when peace comes, you, my son, will be able to talk with our neighbors."

"Do you speak Arabic?" Yusuf asked Sam. "How many Israelis speak the language of the Middle East? Is your family as ignorant as the rest? And maybe I should call you a Jew instead of an Israeli. I am a Palestinian." Yusuf spat out the words.

"There are plenty of Israelis who aren't Jews. And my family is not ignorant—my father is a university professor, though I'm sure you wouldn't know anything about universities. Anyway, Israelis aren't supposed to go into Arab areas, they could be kidnapped or killed, so what do I need to speak Arabic for?"

"My father went to university, and so will I. And you don't need to worry. No Palestinian would kill you, they couldn't be bothered." Yusuf spoke in a low, flat voice.

"Thanks for the reassurance," Sam shot back. "Anyway, why are you in the hospital?"

"I told you, I have an infection in my eye." Yusuf turned his face to the wall.

Sam could just ignore the kid, but how many times did a one-eyed Arab pirate cross one's path? He probably lived in the West Bank, like most Palestinians, although it was possible that he lived in an Arab sector of Jerusalem. Sam looked up at the ceiling. "Where are you from?"

"Plato." Yusuf turned back and stared at the Israeli kid.

"You mean Pluto, and yeah, you're an alien, I got that. How did you lose your eye?"

"An Israeli soldier shot me." Yusuf smiled.

"Israeli soldiers don't miss." Sam turned and grinned at Yusuf. Was there really a hole under that eye-patch? That would be something to see. Pirate Boy's *good* eye didn't look so good either. Sam thought he'd rather have one bad leg than two dud eyes. Besides, there weren't many blind art dealers around, or curators. That's what he liked—art, paintings mostly. There were days when even *he* thought it was weird, which is why he didn't talk about art, paintings, and stuff to anyone except Mr. Rosenthal.

"Israeli soldiers are a bunch of spoiled, alcohol-drinking idiots who are afraid of pregnant women," snapped Yusuf.

"Yeah? And how many pregnant women are actually hiding bombs?"

"That's what I said—your stupid soldiers can't tell a bomb from a baby. Anyway, why are *you* here?" asked Yusuf.

"A suicide bomber got me. I was minding my own business and *boom*! I'm here and the bomber is in a million pieces. I win." Sam threw his hands in the air then flopped backward.

Yusuf sank back into his pillow. He did not believe the Israeli kid. Well, maybe he did, but who cared? He had other things to think about, like the fact that his good eye itched. Yusuf turned his back to Sam and faced the wall. What if he lost sight in his good eye too? Thinking about it made his heart hammer in his chest. He'd rather die than let the Israeli kid see that he was afraid.

CHAPTER 3

❖

Parents, Parents!

S am's mother charged into the hospital room. An overnight bag banged against her hip, while a bulging briefcase dangled from her right hand. Grasped in her left hand was a paper bag with a blue-and-white McDonald's logo on it. Sam sighed. Ima clearly thought that a hamburger would be a big treat. He didn't have the heart to tell her that, really, he didn't care. After all, his mother hated fast food, and yet she had traveled across Jerusalem—only a few of the city's McDonald's served kosher food—just to buy him a kosher hamburger. It was so weird—they didn't keep kosher at home, but in the hospital, for some reason, his mother was suddenly kosher. Anyway, he preferred Burger Ranch, but at the end of the day a Big Mac was a Big Mac, even without the cheese.

Ima rolled his bed tray over and began to pull the food out of the bag. "Is everything all right?" She tipped her head toward his roommate.

Sam looked over at Pirate Boy, who was still doing his glassy-eyed, dead fish imitation, and shrugged. "Sure." What was he supposed to say?

"Here's your phone and charger. It's not completely charged up. Try not to drop this one in the toilet." She passed him the phone, then unwrapped the burger onto a flattened piece of paper. "Ketchup?" she asked. Sam nodded. "And Mr. Rosenthal sent you this." Ima handed him a book.

It was on the art of Ruben Cukier. Sam whistled as he turned the pages, settling on a painting of three stacked heads. He grinned.

"He says that you often go through his collection of art books. Is that true?" Ima looked at him curiously.

Sam nodded without looking up. He flipped through the book. There was a painting called *City of Desire*. The woman in the painting looked a little like Alina, except Alina had blue eyes.

"Mr. Rosenthal would have come himself but he is sitting shivah," said his mother.

"Why? Who died?" Sam looked up.

"His daughter and one of her children were killed on a bus in the territories. What was her name?" Ima spoke without drama, although her bottom lip quivered.

"Hannah," Sam whispered. He felt his fingers go cold, then his hands.

Sam watched his mother. She was fighting tears. Israelis were called *sabras*, like the prickly pear, for a reason: a sabra was rough and tough on the outside but sweet and sensitive on the inside. Really, Ima wasn't all that sweet, but she did care, he knew she did.

His mother took a deep breath then carried on. "Your Great-Aunt Esther is coming to visit you."

"Great-Aunt Esther?" said Sam. They both turned and looked at the Arab kid in the next bed. Great-Aunt Esther was not very tolerant of Arabs, and that was an understatement. "Never forget, Samuel, this land has belonged to us since the beginning of time and will be ours to the end of time," she said in his ear every chance she got.

"I'll make a phone call." Ima grabbed her phone and bolted out into the hall.

Sam held the art book to his chest and then checked the messages on his phone. There were three texts from Alina. *Are you coming?* the last one read. *I'll be in the lobby in an hour.*

"Crisis averted!" Ima flew back into the room. The door closed behind her. "I told Great-Aunt Esther that you were sleeping," his mother whispered in Sam's ear. Sam nodded. Maybe every family had a Great-Aunt Esther.

"Mr. Rosenthal, is he all right?" Sam asked, his eyes back on the book.

Ima shook her head. "The last time he saw his daughter, I don't think it was very pleasant."

Sam remembered the shouting between father and daughter, and he remembered looking into Mr. Rosenthal's garden and seeing his grandchildren, all boys, dressed in dark-colored clothes that looked hot, wearing *kippot* on their heads, their curly hair in sidelocks bouncing beside their ears as they played. "Will you visit him? I mean, if you do, will you thank him for me, for the book, I mean? And will you tell him that I'm sorry about . . . you know, his daughter?" Sam spoke while flipping the pages faster and faster.

"Of course." Ima stared hard at Sam, as if trying to see inside his head.

"Could you turn on the television?" he asked as he put the book aside. He reached for his phone and thumb-texted Alina under the blankets, *Mother on duty*. Sam pushed "Send," slipped the phone under his butt, then looked over at his mother's small overnight bag. "You don't have to stay," he said, a little too casually. His mother had camped out for weeks beside his bed after his accident. His father came occasionally, but he'd arrive late and leave early.

"Your MRI is scheduled for 9:00 a.m., more blood tests and X-rays after that. I will sleep in the chair." As if to make her point, she plopped down in the chair and began shuffling through the files in her briefcase. Ima never went anywhere without her work. She was a curator at Yad Vashem, the Holocaust museum. Ima always talked about the Holocaust as if it had just happened that morning.

A newsreader reported on an explosion at the Rafah border crossing in Gaza. The screen was filled with gray clouds ballooning into the sky.

The door opened. Sam looked up. Pirate Boy had visitors.

"*Habibi*. My darling." Yusuf's mother extended her arms from the doorway. Yusuf pinned his own arms to his side. He didn't have to turn his head to know that the Israeli kid was watching. "Are you all right, my son? Are they treating you well?" Mama cupped her hands around Yusuf's cheeks and waved fluttery fingers over the patch that covered his lost eye. She stood on her toes to reach him in the bed. His mother loomed so large in his mind that he sometimes forgot how tiny she really was. There was a family joke that his grandmother told, "When your Mama gave birth, her babies were bigger than she was!"

"Yes, Mama, I am well," said Yusuf.

"Thanks be to Allah," she answered. Mama wore a long overcoat on top of a long skirt, and a white-and-blue hijab covered her hair. Her eyes could not stay put. She was looking everywhere at once—at the room, the bedding, the walls, but especially at the Israeli woman who sat in the chair by the window. Mama had not been in Jerusalem in many years, not since she was a child, and she had never been inside an Israeli hospital before. Neither she nor Baba had been allowed to come with Yusuf across the border after he was hurt. Up until just recently, the Israelis had been unwilling to issue his parents travel papers.

Baba, quiet and dignified, had followed Mama into the room. "Shalom," he said to the Israeli kid's mother, offering the Hebrew greeting.

"*Assalamu alaykom*," replied the Israeli kid's mother. Yusuf caught a look from the Israeli kid. Was Yusuf surprised that Sam's mother could speak a few words of Arabic? Yusuf's father pulled the privacy curtain along the thin silver curtain rod. It caught halfway. Maybe Baba should speak Russian to it, he thought, and smiled.

Yusuf's mother was saying, "We were at the border crossing for eight hours. Another bomb went off. But no matter, we are here now, Allah be praised. We have a forty-eight-hour transit pass. Imagine! Your father and I will stay with Uncle Yamen in El-Quds, in Wadi el-Joz, tonight."

Yusuf's father plopped a large red cooler on the hospital-bed tray. As Mama talked, she lined up a row of plastic containers across the tray. Yusuf was not about to tell her that he liked the hospital food, especially the soft white buns. Anyway, Israeli food was almost like their own. The largest container was filled with hummus topped with olive oil and pine nuts. The small containers held olives, pickles, baba ghanoush, pickled cucumber, a cheese called *jibneh baida*, Mama's homemade pita bread, and his favorite, *bakdoonsiyyeh*, a tomato salad. Mama would have spent most of the day making the food, and his grandmother would have filled the plastic containers and stacked them in the cooler.

"How did you get all this across the border?" Yusuf asked.

Mama glanced over at the Israeli boy and his mother and shook her head.

"Mama, they don't speak Arabic. You can say whatever you want," Yusuf whispered.

Still, Mama shook her head as she unwrapped a small pile of bread. Mama believed that walls had ears.

"Mama." Wait, why was *he* whispering? "Did Mira get into university?" His sister Mira, who lived for studying, who wanted to be a dentist, who dreamed of attending university, should have heard by now. Mama looked toward Baba. What did that look mean? Did Mira not get into school because of him? Was it because he was in an Israeli hospital? Were they calling him a collaborator? "Mama, tell me."

"Eat, eat, Yusuf." Mama rolled the tray closer.

"But Mama, they give us food here," said Yusuf.

"Pah! This hospital food will not get you well. Eat!" said Mama.

Baba, standing at the end of the bed, handed Yusuf a small brown bag. He looked tall and serious in a crisp white shirt, black pants with a black belt, and well-shined leather shoes. "And this is from your uncle." Baba's eyes twinkled.

"Thank you," said Yusuf as he peeked into the bag. It was caramels from Jafar's, the oldest candy shop in the Old City. The Old City was a city within a city, a mysterious ancient place tucked into the new city of Jerusalem. How he wanted to see the candy shop, the holy places, *everything* in the Old City.

Baba must have read his mind because he said softly, "Wait, my son. You will see the Old City of Jerusalem with your very own eyes one day. Just be patient."

Patient? Yusuf could see the walls of the Old City right outside his hospital window. There were times when he just wanted to jump out the window and run.

"I brought your glasses. You forgot them again." Mama held up the ugly, black-rimmed glasses that had belonged to his dead uncle. Yusuf wrinkled his nose and looked over at Sam. The privacy curtain hid everything but the Israeli kid's feet and the Big Mac sitting on the edge of the tray. He caught his father looking at the McDonald's bag too. Baba had a sucking-lemons look on his face.

Sam looked over at the Arab family. He couldn't see Pirate Boy's mother, but his father was in view. He looked green, like he was scared something might happen to the kid. Didn't Palestinians all have twenty kids? The father looked at his son sadly. No, not sadly, with affection! If their kids were so precious, why did they send them out into the streets to heave rocks at Israeli tanks? Every night, Sam saw Palestinians on the news shouting at the television cameras. Some of them even brought their kids along. They shook their fists, spewing insults and screaming threats of retribution. They had really bad teeth. This man didn't seem at all like that. He seemed, well, normal.

CHAPTER 4

❖

Come Back Tomorrow

"Are you finished with your hamburger?" Without waiting for an answer, Sam's mother swept away the paper debris and tidied his tray. Ima hated cleaning at home, but in the hospital she was fastidious about everything. He was pretty sure that she had ironed his underwear.

Sam's phone vibrated. Alina's name popped up. *"Coffee asap."* He glanced up at the television as his mother flipped through a binder, checking, back-checking, the pages softly brushing against one another. How was he going to get rid of her?

"Shalom."

Startled, Sam looked up to see his father standing at the foot of his bed. Abba's mouth was pursed tight, his forehead furrowed. He looked uncomfortable.

"Such a surprise. What are you doing here?" Ima got the question out first.

"I have come to wish my son well tomorrow." Abba spoke quietly. He seemed concerned. Why? Sam followed his father's line of vision. Pirate Boy's father also stood at the bottom of his son's bed. The two men were only a short distance apart. Sam glanced from one to the other. They looked alike, both standing tall and erect. No one spoke. He could hear Pirate Boy's mother murmur something in Arabic. The air was thick and heavy. And then Abba turned to face Pirate Boy's father. Sam sucked in a breath.

"I hope your son is comfortable," said Abba.

Pirate Boy's father nodded. "Thank you. He is."

Sam let out a slow breath. Except for a voice on the television in the background, the room was still quiet, but it was a different quiet.

"The cleaners will be here in a few minutes. You must leave soon." Tuba-Luba's voice smashed through the silence like a rock fired through glass. She flicked on the overhead lights and instantly the room was flooded with a sick shade of blue. In an odd way, Sam was actually glad to see her.

Luba pushed a little tray on wheels into the room. She stopped at the foot of Yusuf's bed. Yusuf's parents were squished up against the lockers.

Without explanation, Luba unscrewed a small container and held up a dropper. Yusuf knew the drill. He put his head back on the pillow and waited for the drops to fall into his eye. They landed like raindrops—*ping, ping, ping.* He could hear the sound not through his ears, but through his eye. Next Luba doled out pills, which Yusuf swallowed. There was a trick to it—back of the tongue, gulp. Until he had come to this hospital he had never swallowed a pill in his whole life.

"They will help with the pain. As soon as the test results are back you will begin a new course of intravenous antibiotics."

Yusuf nodded as Luba wrote hieroglyphics in a medical chart. The nurse barely acknowledged his parents. His mother's eyes were wide and her hands were clenched into two hard balls. She looked terrified.

"Mama, it's all right," he said in Arabic. His mother nodded, but the expression on her face did not change.

Tuba-Luba marched toward Sam, batted the curtain back, and announced, "You will also begin a new course of antibiotics in the morning." In that same tone of voice she might have said, "You will be taken out at dawn and executed by firing squad."

Sam understood. Both he and Pirate Boy were here for tests and rounds of intravenous meds. That explained why they were in the same room. Sam swallowed his own pills as Tuba-Luba marched off to make someone else's life miserable.

"I bet she worked in a jail in Russia. What are they called? Gulags?" Sam muttered.

"Shush," said his mother, but by the pull of her mouth and the furrow of her brow it was clear that she was annoyed at the nurse's abruptness too.

"I will say good night," said Abba.

Why had he come? They hadn't said more than two words to each other. That's the way it was with them now, though it hadn't always been like that. When Sam was little, he and Abba had walked the Judean Hills collecting fossils almost every Saturday afternoon. But that was before Sam's aunt was killed. Her death had changed everything.

"Ima, you should go home with Abba." Sam tried to keep the eagerness out of his voice. He looked toward his father hoping for backup. None came.

Sam's mother closed the locks on her briefcase: *snap, snap*, like small firecrackers going off.

"Ima, please. You don't have to stay here tonight." Sam's voice was about to pitch into a whine. He stopped himself. He was so sick of being treated like a child but he didn't need Pirate Boy hearing him sound like one.

His mother paused, looked over at her husband, then gave Sam one of those quizzical *I'm not sure what you are up to* looks. "I have already arranged to take tomorrow off work." Her voice had a waffling sound to it.

"Perhaps Sam is right. We could both come back to-morrow morning," said Abba.

Sam nodded his head a bit too vigorously. "Really, I'm fine. And you know how lousy you feel when you sleep sitting up." It was a last-ditch effort. His father looked uncomfortable, his mother dithered, and his phone vibrated under the blanket—all at the same time. Sam pushed the phone farther under his butt. "Come back tomorrow," he said.

"Well, I doubt that you can get into any trouble with that nurse on duty." His mother sighed.

What trouble? Since when did he get into any trouble? Okay, twice he and Alina had stayed up talking all night in the bomb shelter. When they'd turned up in the morning all they'd got was a lecture from the nurse on duty. Big deal.

His mother began packing up her notes and binders. "Do you want this on?" She motioned toward the television. Sam shook his head. Ima paused. It looked as though she was about to speak to the Arabs, maybe ask them they wanted to watch television, but instead she picked up the remote and turned the television off.

Ima planted a kiss on Sam's forehead, something she would not normally have done. "We will be back first thing in the morning," she said while gathering her briefcase and purse. And then she added, "*Smokh aleinu*." She was always saying that—"Rely on us." Rely on them for what?

Abba mumbled a good night, and they were gone, or almost gone. Ima paused again at the doorway. "Good night," she said to Pirate Boy's mother. The woman looked confused at first and then nodded. Within moments Pirate Boy's parents left too.

Sam swallowed a cheer. The night was about to begin.

CHAPTER 5

✜

Escape

S am swung his legs out of bed. He meant to land on his left foot but touched down on both feet instead. The sting in his right ankle shot up his backbone and lodged somewhere in his head. His foot jerked upward as if burned. Yelping, he clutched the flannel sheets and thin blanket. *Breathe, breathe.* Sam sucked in air as he gingerly lowered himself to the ground, shifting his weight onto his good leg.

That was interesting, Yusuf thought as he watched the Israeli kid hop around on one foot. The ankle was not only swollen but also red and shiny.

"You called Luba a Merkava. I heard you. Do you know Israeli tanks?" Sam asked as he made for one of the lockers at the bottom of the bed. The pill Tuba-Luba had doled out was reducing the pain in his leg, but not fast enough.

"Sure, your soldiers use them to tear down our homes." Yusuf shrugged.

"Tanks don't do that," said Sam, although really he was guessing. He pulled on his pants, inching the right pant leg carefully over his ankle.

"Sorry, D9 bulldozers destroy our homes," snapped Yusuf. He reached into the bag of candy and popped a caramel into his mouth. Delicious.

"Maybe if you stop blowing us up, we'll stop mowing down your houses," Sam shot back.

"I could have called her a T-90," said Yusuf.

Sam was hardly listening. He looked at his ankle and leg critically. What if one day his foot wasn't there? What if they really did amputate? Thinking about it made his heart hammer and his hands shake. Sam did up his belt. "What did you say?" he asked, not that he cared much.

"I said that she looks like a T-90. That's a Russian third-generation battle tank made of steel and nickel thicker than an Israeli's skull," said Yusuf.

"The Merkava is better," said Sam. He picked up his phone and googled "Merkava." He read out loud, "'The exact type of armor is kept classified, but it is known to be extremely tough. All Merkava models have excellent armored protection.'" Sam smiled.

Yusuf reached into the candy bag, popped another

candy, then jumped out of bed and stood looking over Sam's shoulder. "Google 'Russian tanks,'" he said.

Sam paused. How did an Arab kid know about Google? He could smell the candy.

A list of Russian tanks popped up. Squinting, Yusuf pointed to the top of the list.

"'It features a new generation of Kontakt-5 explosive reactive armor on its hull and turret,'" Sam read out.

"That's Luba, she has reactive armor . . ." said Yusuf.

"That can kill." Sam nodded.

"With one glance from her laser eyes," added Yusuf.

"And sausage breath," replied Sam.

"Her breath is a Russian secret weapon."

"How do you know stuff about tanks?" Sam asked. He really was curious.

"How else? The Internet," replied Yusuf as he climbed back into his bed. What if he offered the Israeli kid a candy? He looked back at Sam and changed his mind. Why should he?

Sam pursed his lips. He kept turning over in his head all the images he had of Palestinians: scrappy, dirty children; screaming women, all beaks and chins, dressed like vampires but with vibrating tongues; bellowing men with stubby, rotting teeth hammering the sky with clenched fists; desolate land dotted with dying trees, cement houses crumbling into dust, and giant concrete barriers blocking roads. He didn't think that more than a few could read, let alone use the Internet.

"I think Luba looks like that Greek goddess that has snakes for hair," said Sam as he perched on the edge of the bed. Enough of this. Alina was waiting.

"Medusa," said Yusuf. "And she wasn't a goddess, she was a mortal. That's how come she was murdered."

Sam tried not to look amazed. How did this guy know about Greek mythology? He opened his mouth to ask but then thought of Alina. Sam rolled on ankle socks, slipped on the blue-and-white padded shoe, and wiggled his other foot into a running shoe. Pirate Boy was watching; he could feel it. How much could he see out of one eye?

"Where are you going?" Yusuf was curious—not insanely curious, not wildly curious, just bored curious.

"None of your business," snapped Sam. He checked the time on his phone. It took the cleaners about an hour to clean the rooms, and after that there was a shift change, and an hour after that was bed check. Bed checks were no big deal. Once the lights were out all the staff did was open the door, peek in, and close it again.

Sam reached for a book on the table that separated their beds. He kept 80 shekels hidden in its pages. Shoving the bills in his pocket he felt an old *kippah*. For some

inexplicable reason, his mother liked him to keep one handy.
He pushed it deeper into his pocket.

Next, the bed. Sam pushed one of his pillows under the
sheet and threw the blanket overtop, then stuffed a sock
with a facecloth and dangled it out the bottom. He stood
back, fluffed the bedding, stood back, adjusted the foot,
stood back, and nodded with satisfaction. It would work, as
long as Luba (a.k.a. Tuba/Merkava/Medusa) did not flick on
the overhead lights. Yusuf watched the show with interest.

Hopping from the bed to the locker, Sam grabbed his
metal crutches. Then before he took off he stopped on the
threshold and looked up and down the empty hall. "See ya,"
he said over his shoulder as he stepped out into the hall and
took a quick right.

Yusuf heard the crash. It was tempting to just lie on his
bed and laugh, but he had to see this for himself. He leaped
out of bed and peeked out into the hall and around the
corner. A rope lay across Sam's chest, and his head rested on
a plastic DANGER sign.

Yusuf covered his mouth with his hand to smother the
laughter. "Need help?" he finally asked.

Sam should have felt humiliated, but instead he felt
loopy. His head wobbled *no*.

Shrugging, Yusuf walked back into the room and stood
between the beds long enough to feel guilty. There was

a hospital wheelchair across the hall. He could see it. He walked out of the room, past Sam, and pulled the wheelchair over. He stood behind it and didn't say a word.

"I don't need that," Sam snarled as he struggled to sit up. Embarrassment had set in.

"Fine. I'll ring for the Tank." Yusuf shrugged.

"No!" Sam cried out, louder than he had intended. He peered down the hall. Not a nurse in sight. If he was caught wearing his street clothes his parents would certainly be phoned.

"Chair?" Smiling, Yusuf motioned to the wheelchair.

"Piss off," Sam snarled in English while wiggling over to the chair.

"That's your favorite English expression, isn't it?" Yusuf smiled. It was his favorite English expression too.

Sam put his hands on the arms of the chair and heaved. "Aggggggh." An involuntary old-man grunt erupted out of his mouth. The chair rolled back. Sam slipped and hit the floor.

Letting out a loud, dramatic sigh, Yusuf stood behind Sam, put his arms under Sam's armpits, and heaved. *One*, *two*, *three*: Yusuf threw Sam into the chair like he was landing a fish in a boat. But the brake still wasn't on. The wheelchair shot across the hall and banged into the opposite wall. Sam, propped up in the chair like a doll, lurched forward, then fell back.

"Are you trying to kill me?" he muttered.

"You are doing a great job on your own." Yusuf walked back to the room. So much for being helpful.

"Shut up," Sam snarled after him.

"You shut up," Yusuf called over his shoulder.

The crutches were on the other side of some paint cans. Sam picked up a short board from the debris and made a stab at retrieving them, but he only made matters worse. One crutch slipped behind all the junk, and the other became wedged against the wall. A door opened down the hall. Sam spun the chair around and backed into the wall. On a second try he rolled into his room, took a breath, and sat for a moment. The chair was harder to maneuver than it looked.

"Sorry," Sam mumbled.

"Sorry for what? What do you want?" Yusuf was suspicious.

"What do you mean?" Sam played innocent.

Yusuf hopped up on his bed and looked up at the ceiling. The pain in his head had dissipated. The medication was working.

Sam thought for a moment. "I'm meeting someone on the first floor. My crutches . . . if you help, I'll . . ." What did he have that an Arab kid would want? "I'll buy you a cola. There's a machine in the lobby." Likely Pirate Boy only drank that muddy coffee they served at falafel stands.

It was disgusting stuff that smelled like burnt rubber. Still, Yusuf said nothing. Time was ticking. "And I'll buy you a bag of Bamba."

Peanut-flavored puffs were his favorite junk food. Yusuf folded his hands behind his head.

"Do you want to lie here all night or *do* something?" Sam was getting desperate.

Yusuf sat up. "Why do you want to go to the first floor so badly?"

"I told you, I'm meeting someone," said Sam.

"Who?" asked Yusuf.

"A friend."

"Why doesn't he come to the room?" Yusuf smelled a rat.

"He is a *she*," said Sam. All this talk was chewing up precious time.

"You know a girl?" The word 'girl' vibrated up his throat and almost exploded out of his mouth. No Palestinian boy would dare meet a girl without a chaperone. Not that they all didn't dream about girls and the kinds of relationships they saw on European and American television shows.

Sam looked at Yusuf as if he had two heads. "Alina is a *friend*. She was a tennis pro, almost, before she got sick. Anyway, it's none of your business. Do you want to come or not?" All he really needed was the crutches, although getting pushed around in a wheelchair would be better than crashing into everything.

"But it's after visiting hours."

"She's not a visitor. Alina is a patient." Sam swiveled the wheelchair around, bashed into the bottom of Yusuf's bed, rolled back, hit his bed, then rolled toward the door. "Are you coming or not?"

"They don't let you drive a car, do they?" asked Yusuf, his mouth pursed as if holding in a laugh.

"I'm fourteen." Sam looked at the time on his phone.

Yusuf made up his mind suddenly. "Yes." He launched himself toward the cupboard as if sprung from a catapult, yanked on his pants and shirt, rolled on socks, slipped his feet into his running shoes, and pulled a thin wool sweater over his head. It had come out of a charity bundle from Australia. The sweater was blue and had the word "Socceroos" on the sleeve. He paused, then shoved his uncle's ugly glasses into one pocket and the bag of caramel candy into the other.

"Your bed—fix it," Sam told him. Yusuf snatched his pillows and shaped them into a body, of sorts. "The lights," Sam said. Yusuf flicked them off.

Both stuck their heads out into the hall and looked up and down. Sam could see the nurses sitting in a glassed-in office behind the nursing station. "There." Sam pointed to the crutches on the other side of the debris.

"Hang on." Yusuf gave the wheelchair a mighty shove. Sam sailed down the hall, stifling a scream, as Yusuf scooped up the crutches and ran after him.

The chair was careening toward the nursing station. *Brakes! Brakes! Brakes!* "Jeeeeeze," Sam complained just as Yusuf grabbed the handles of the chair. A split second later and Sam would have smashed into the half-wall that divided the station from the hallway. "Idiot!" Breathing hard, Sam reached out and took a swipe at Yusuf, who ducked and grinned. Both huddled against the wall.

"What are they doing?" Sam whispered.

Yusuf peeked over the half-wall. The nurses were sitting around a table behind the glass window. "Talking," he whispered back. The elevator was close by, in full view of the nursing station. "Wait here." Yusuf bolted down the hall, slammed his hand against the elevator button, and suddenly tried to look casual, as if he were a late visitor leaving the ward.

Wait here? Where else would he go? Party? Dance? Sam stood the crutches up on the footrests. He could walk to the elevator now. What did he need Pirate Boy for? *One, two*—he rocked back in the chair. The door to the nursing station opened. In that moment, between open and closed, Sam could hear the nurses' voices quite plainly.

"Yusuf Senad, the Arab boy, has displayed signs of infection around the implant of his left eye. He may lose sight in his good eye if the infection cannot be controlled by antibiotics. The infection may also spread to the brain. It could have been handled easily in the beginning but he was sent home to the West Bank two weeks ago and was not allowed to cross back until this morning. He is on oral antibiotics at the moment and was given pain medication an hour ago. His blood work should be back soon and he will begin a course of intravenous antibiotics at 7:00 a.m. He is currently on . . ." The door closed.

Sam slumped back in the wheelchair. He looked up to see Pirate Boy coming toward him.

"Hang on." Yusuf spun around the back of the chair and shoved it toward the open elevator. Sam, clutching the crutches, did as he was told.

CHAPTER 6

❖

Alina

They rode the elevator in silence. The words "the infection may also spread to the brain" banged around in Sam's head. Did Pirate Boy know how sick he was? They weren't friends. It wasn't like he could say anything to the kid . . . and anyway, what would he say?

No one paid them any attention when they rolled out of the elevator onto the first floor. Two Arab nurses wearing white headscarves brushed past them. They were speaking in Arabic and giggling. Sam rolled his eyes. Why did girls giggle so much? With the exception of two bored security guys armed with clipboards and small sidearms, the place was almost empty.

Yusuf pushed the wheelchair across a large Star of David inlaid in the floor. Only Sam looked down. It was a memorial to the armored convoy of medical people who were attacked during the 1948 Arab–Israeli War, when Israel first became a state. Seventy-nine people, mostly doctors and nurses, were murdered by Arabs. Sam might have said, "Hey, Pirate Boy, given another chance, your people would slaughter the same people that are saing your eyesight now," but he didn't feel like it anymore. Maybe they couldn't save his eyesight. Maybe they couldn't save him.

"Over here." Alina, dressed in skinny jeans and a purple shirt, and holding on to the medical pole, waved from across the lobby. Yusuf stopped in his tracks. The wheelchair came to an abrupt halt.

"Stop that! I'm getting whiplash. What's wrong with you?" Sam looked over his shoulder. Yusuf's mouth was shaped into a big fat "O." He followed Yusuf's line of vision. "What? Never seen a pink-haired girl before?" Sam put his hands on the wheels and rolled the wheelchair forward under his own steam.

Alina had changed wigs. And she wore a matching pink T-shirt with English words on it. He could make out the word "life" but the rest was a mystery.

"What are you doing in that?" Alina pointed to the chair but she was looking at Yusuf.

"Got myself a pusher." Sam motioned toward Yusuf, who had trailed behind.

Yusuf did not know where to look. He gazed down at the floor, the wall, a passing male orderly. She had blue eyes. Some of the Israeli soldiers who came into his city had blue eyes. When he was little he'd thought that men with blue eyes saw the world in blue. Even with blue eyes and pink hair, she was the most beautiful girl he had ever seen.

"Hi." Alina smiled at Yusuf.

"Meet my new roommate, Yusuf the Pirate. He keeps a parrot, and enjoys the occasional keg of rum and attacking defenseless ships on the high seas." Sam spoke while struggling to stand up on his crutches.

"*Marhaba*, Yusuf. My name is Alina."

She'd said hello in Arabic. And her voice had a singsong quality to it. "Sh-Sh-Shalom," Yusuf stammered.

"A stuttering pirate," Sam muttered.

"Sam, don't be mean." Alina gave Sam a gentle poke without taking her eyes off Yusuf. "Do you speak Hebrew?" she asked Yusuf sweetly.

"Yes, I speak He-He-Hebrew," replied Yusuf. His face grew hot, and the tips of his ears were scalding.

Sam scowled. Alina smiled.

"You do recall that he's the rocket-building, rock-throwing, suicide-bomber type." Sam was joking, but not really. And why was the guy stuttering all of a sudden?

Alina ignored him. "Didn't you promise me a coffee?"

she asked Sam. "Wait, Yusuf, maybe you would like a cola instead of coffee? Our coffee is not as strong as yours." Alina was speaking gently.

"Thank you." Yusuf nodded.

Sam's head swiveled from side to side. What was going on here? He sat down and rolled the chair toward the vending machines while puffing out air like a small engine. At least she had switched back to Hebrew.

Four little wheels rattled behind the wheelchair as Alina pushed her medical pole along the tiled floor. She reached out every few steps to grab the back of a chair or the wall to steady herself. Yusuf looked at the bag that hung on the pole and the plastic tube and needle that were taped to her arm.

And then, as if she could read his mind, she said, "I have stage-four cancer. T-cell lymphoma. I've done the chemo-therapy thing. I come in for blood transfusions once a week, sometimes twice. Just call me Dracula." Yusuf thought she spoke as if she were reading from a script. In the West Bank, having cancer usually meant death. But she didn't *sound* like she had cancer, she was too happy. And who was Dracula?

"There's nothing that can be done," Alina carried on. "Well, there is one thing—a stem cell transplant. But first the cancer has to be stabilized, and the stem cell transplant is a long process. It's not like they just take a needle and shoot cells in. My mother spends every waking minute on the Internet trying to find alternative therapies, and my father has suddenly become all religious. He's all, you know, about life, and all that stuff. We Jews go nuts at a wedding because it's about life and the possibility of new life. Now a Jewish funeral is something else. Everyone moans and groans. Why bother? I mean, it's not like anyone is getting out of this world alive. I'm talking too much. I always talk too much." She laughed again.

Yusuf had never heard such a laugh. His sisters did not laugh like that. He tried to steady himself to make his heart stop pounding. He lowered his voice and made an attempt at being serious. "Your shirt." Yusuf motioned to her T-shirt. And then he had a thought, a horrible thought! Blood rushed to his cheeks and ears. Did she think he was looking at her . . .?

"Oh, this? Do you speak English?" she asked. Yusuf shook his head. "It says, 'Life Takes Time.'" Alina translated into Hebrew while holding out her shirt with her fingertips, making her breasts disappear. "A friend of mine came up with it, it's kind of our slogan. It means that time *is* life, but I guess, in the end, time takes life." Alina shrugged.

"In . . . in . . . in my faith, we must live a good life so that we will spend eternity with Allah, the Creator." Yusuf swallowed hard.

Alina leaned her head to one side. "Do you ever wonder why so many Jews and Muslims hate each other? I mean, don't we have the same God? Different names, of course.

And Abraham was our common ancestor. Christians too, right? And yet all we do is fight. Do you think that it's because Jews are all about life, and Muslims are about"—she paused—"afterlife?"

Yusuf nodded. But maybe he should have shaken his head? He was confused. *Say something, anything!* "My father says that your King David is our Daoud, the emperor and servant of Allah." Was that right? His mouth felt like it was packed with straw. Wait, he hadn't stuttered.

"Do you know what I *really* think?" Alina smiled shyly. Yusuf stood, tongue-tied and transfixed. "I think we're all trying to be God's favorite children, and God doesn't play favorites." Alina giggled.

What should he do now? It was hard to concentrate on what she was saying. Could she hear his heart thumping? He was getting sweaty. She was so beautiful. Her eyes . . . the way she stood. Wait, was he standing too close?

"This machine took my money," Sam hollered from a distance as he rolled over to talk to the two guards at the front door.

"I'm pretty sure those guys aren't going to help." Alina pointed to the guards. "I bet Sam's going to ask them to find the repair guy—at this time of night!" She smiled at Yusuf. "I know what you're thinking." His mouth fell open. Could she read his mind? His eyes fell to the floor. He felt sick.

"You're thinking that I sound like an old history teacher. That's the trouble with being sick, we spend too much time with adults, too much time reading, and way too much time thinking. There's a six-year-old girl with bone cancer on my ward, cute little thing. She talks like a rabbi."

Breathe, breathe. What was she saying?

"But maybe it's not just cancer that makes us sound old. Maybe it's everything, you know, like living in the Middle East. Or maybe it's the same way in any war zone— of course, no one calls Israel a war zone! Who would holiday in a war zone?" Alina smiled a little sadly. "But every time we step out of the house our parents worry that we're going to get blown up or something."

Yusuf nodded. "My mother worries all the time too."

"Really? Does she?" Alina looked at him, wide-eyed.

"She worries more about my brother," Yusuf carried on. "He has a temper. There are too many Palestinian boys in prison for throwing rocks at the Israeli military convoys. She worries that he may go to prison one day." He'd said three, maybe four whole sentences without stuttering.

"I'm sorry," Alina said softly.

"About what?" He was curious. He had never thought that an Israeli could be sorry about anything, but everything about her was unexpected. He looked over at Sam and the guards. One of the guards was talking on a phone.

"Your eye . . . What happened?" There was no pity in her face, just interest.

"There was"—he paused—"an accident." Yusuf fingered the caramels in his pocket. Did she like sweets? Should he offer her one? What if she said no? Maybe sweets were not on her diet. Did people with cancer have special diets?

"Have you been to this hospital before?" Alina changed the subject.

"I've been at the other campus, the one in Ein Kerem. That's where they did the surgery. They sent me here for tests and treatment. I like it here. I can see the Old City from my window." The caramels were melting in his pocket. Yusuf dithered and then, deep breath, "Would you like one? They are from Jafar's." He held out the bag.

"That's the shop in the Old City, right? They have amazing candy." She reached into the bag and pulled out a caramel.

"You have been to the Old City, the Arab section?" Yusuf was amazed.

"Lots of times," she said simply.

"I would like to go too," replied Yusuf.

"Really? Then why don't you?" As soon as the words were out of her mouth Alina felt the blood rush to her face. "I'm sorry. I'm really . . ." Of course he couldn't go where he pleased. He was not an Arab Israeli, he was from the West Bank. He needed permission and travel papers to walk around Israel. He was not even allowed outside the hospital. She knew that.

"The machine's broken and they can't find the maintenance guy," Sam said while rolling closer to them. He'd heard bits of their conversation: *Jafar's*, *candy shop*, *Old City*.

"It doesn't matter. We don't need anything to drink." Alina tucked a strand of pink hair behind her ear as Sam stopped and put on the brake.

"I know where the other machine is," said Yusuf.

"Really, it's okay." Alina smiled.

Sam watched as Yusuf shifted from foot to foot. Both Alina and Yusuf were eating candy. The fact that Pirate Boy had not offered him a candy did not go unnoticed.

Yusuf reached past Alina, snatched the money from Sam's open hand, and took off down the hall. Sam watched, astonished. Pirate Boy was behaving like he was on a quest from what's-her-name, King Arthur's wife, Guinevere—the one who cheated on Arthur with Lancelot. Well, Pirate Boy was no Sir Lancelot, and he was no King Arthur.

"That's the last we'll see of my money," said Sam. He was oddly pleased.

"That's not fair, Sam."

"So, you're on their side now?"

"Does that mean that I don't believe that every Palestinian is out to kill me?" Alina sounded fierce.

"So, it's okay with you that the Arabs blow us up?" He

was getting a bit peeved. Not that he believed for a second that Pirate Boy was a threat, at least not to his safety.

"You think that *he* will kill us?"

"No, I think that he just stole my money."

"He didn't steal anything. He's gone to get drinks, and when he comes back you will say you're sorry." Alina swallowed the candy.

"Sorry for what? That I love my country and that my country is Israel?" Sam tried not to sound defensive. It wasn't working.

"Really, is the radio on? You sound like one of those stupid phone-in shows. Does that mean that the only way to love Israel is to hate Palestine? Or the only way to be a good Israeli is to hate Palestinians? Is that what is supposed to bind us together—hatred?" Suddenly Alina looked tired, really tired. She was tiny to begin with but now she seemed to be shrinking, almost deflating! Sam stopped himself from saying anything more.

"Sam, don't be mad. But don't you get it, I mean, how they feel? Leaving their land, their farms, their homes when it was decided that this country was going to be Israel? I was just thinking, how would you like it if your family had to run from your house to avoid a war you didn't want, and then you couldn't go back afterward?"

Sam crossed his arms and rested his chin on his chest. Was he supposed to feel sorry for people who lobbed bombs a couple of times a day over the borders whenever they felt like it? Was he supposed to care about people who actually *said* that they wanted Jews out of Israel so badly that they should all be driven into the sea? It was so bad that Israel had to put up a security barrier to separate Israel from the West Bank and keep the terrorists on the other side. And since the walls had gone up, hadn't there been fewer bombing incidents? Sam scoffed as he fiddled with the brake on the wheelchair.

"The Arabs can leave anytime they want. They can go to America or Egypt or Jordan or anywhere. Anyway, it's not like we have control over what happens to us. They are the ones who keep bombing us." Sam looked down at his leg.

"Sam, forget about who did what to whom. I'm talking about one guy, Yusuf. He wants to see Jerusalem. Why is it such a big deal? I don't want to fight with you," she said.

"Here." Yusuf came around the corner holding up two colas. "The other machine was out of change so I went to the cafeteria. It's closed, but a supervisor gave me these for free. There was no coffee. Here's your money back."

Sam did not have to look at Alina to know she was smiling. Damn again.

Alina took the drink. "*Shukran*," she said.

Shukran? How come she was speaking Arabic again? Sam was positively seething. He took the other cola.

"Where is your drink?" she asked.

Yusuf shook his head, "I don't like fizzy drinks."

"What are you, six? The word is *carbonated*, not fizzy."
Sam was getting snarly.

"Sam!" Alina stamped her foot just as her phone rang.
She pulled it out of her back pocket and, walking a few steps
away, answered it. "Shalom."

Sam watched. She was unsteady on her feet. Forget
Pirate Boy, Alina was getting sicker.

She jammed the phone back into her pocket while
walking toward them. "That was Tamanna, my roommate.
My nurse is looking for me. I have to go."

"Is she Russian?" Sam and Yusuf both spoke at once.

Alina looked from one to the other. "No, one nurse is
Arab and the other is Australian. They're both nice. Why?"

"Nothing." Again, they spoke in unison, like little kids.

"I'm not sure what you two are up to, but I have to go."
She took a gulp of pop, then held out her hand.

Yusuf looked at it. A Muslim boy was not supposed to
touch a girl who was not a close relative.

"It was good meeting you, Yusuf." She smiled again.
Yusuf reached out and shook her hand. It was cold but her
grip was strong. "Maybe I'll see you tomorrow night. I
have a really cute white wig, very Lady Gaga." She laughed
again. Yusuf grinned. "Bye, Sam." She waved and then
suddenly, unexpectedly, leaned over and gave Sam a peck on

the cheek. But it wasn't a kiss, it was an excuse to whisper, "Be nice—for me?"

Sam watched as she disappeared around the corner, except she was so thin she almost disappeared *before* she turned the corner. He dumped the can into the garbage, stood up on his crutches, and wobbled toward the elevator.

"Wait. Don't you want to ride in the wheelchair?" Yusuf called out after him.

"Get lost," Sam muttered.

"You are angry and I do not know why." Yusuf pushed the empty chair toward the elevator.

"You're a poser," Sam sneered.

"I do not understand that word," Yusuf replied.

"*Po-ssss-errrr.*" Sam pronounced the word slowly. "It's an English word. It means that you just pretend stuff. You were flirting your face off."

Yusuf stood, stunned. Flirting?

The elevator door opened. She stood in a thin overcoat —stout and solid as a bull. First there was surprise—eyes rounded, eyebrows pinned to her forehead, mouth open wide enough to catch flies, nostrils flaring—and then, like a howling wind, "Why are you not in bed?" Tuba-Luba stepped off the elevator and bellowed into Sam's face. "You think this is hotel and you come and go as you please? It is always the same with you Israeli boys. You are spoiled. Your parents give you everything because you must join the army at eighteen. It is honor to protect country. In Russia, boys like you would get good beating for misbehaving." She jutted out her chin and turned her wrath on Yusuf. "And you are guest in this country. You follow rules or you go back to where you come from."

Yusuf just looked down at his shoes but Sam could barely contain his anger. Who did she think she was? Sam opened his mouth.

"*Nyet*! You say nothing." She lifted a finger and pointed it in Sam's face. "You go back to your bed and stay there. You want I should take you back myself?"

Two young, giggling nurses stepped out from behind Tuba-Luba. Embarrassment, anger, and humiliation welled up in Sam and threatened to drown him. How dare she? He shook his head and turned. Everyone in the lobby, even the guards by the door, was laughing.

Tuba-Luba brushed between them, marched past the guards, pushed open the exit door, and plunged into the night.

"Come on." Sam could barely speak, he was so angry.

"Where are we going?" Yusuf dithered. "What should I do with the chair?"

"Leave it." Sam moved on his crutches with surprising speed and grace.

Following in Luba's footsteps, Sam and Yusuf passed the guards.

Stepping outside the air-conditioned hospital was like running full blast into a wall of heat. Spotlights pooled on the large, open plaza, illuminating huge pots of flowers. Twisted metal sculptures appeared menacing in the dark. Ambulance sirens wailed in the distance. Two hairless, skinny cats with fishy eyes and miniature doggy-ears patrolled the court. Beyond, and lit up in colored lights, was the walled city of Jerusalem, the 'city of peace,' which was kind of stupid, Sam thought, when you realized that it had never known any lasting peace. He could see Tuba-Luba, in the far parking lot under the streetlights, getting into her car. *May all your teeth fall out—except one, so you can have a toothache.* That was one of Great-Aunt Esther's curses. She had a million.

Sam turned and looked at the Arab kid. "How much can you actually see?"

"What's it to you?" Yusuf was angry too. Did the Israeli kid think he was the only one offended by Luba-the-Tank's comments? How could he be a "guest" in his own land?

"Can you see the parking lot?" Sam asked, not particularly nicely.

Yusuf fingered his uncle's ugly glasses in his pocket but didn't take them out. Truthfully, he couldn't see much in the dark except the lights, and they were only fuzzy orbs. Yusuf tried not to squint as he reasoned it out. Soldiers would be in the parking lot. They came in twos. They would approach incoming cars, check identification if necessary, and pull the car apart if they felt like it. He knew all this from experience.

"There are two soldiers down there and they have assault riffles hanging off them," said Yusuf. All soldiers carried some sort of guns, usually rifles.

Sam nodded and asked, "Look at me. Can you see my face clearly?"

"Yes. You are ugly." Yusuf smiled. Up close he could see everything, but a bit farther away, not as much.

"So are you. Do you know where this candy shop is? The one called Jafar's?" Sam tried to sound flippant.

"I know that it's in the Old City. Why?" asked Yusuf.

"Alina likes the candy, that's all. We could go." A plan was beginning to form in Sam's mind.

Yusuf was shocked. Was he thinking of leaving the hospital? "What do you mean? You think I should apply for an escort to take me out?" He tilted his head and looked at Sam quizzically.

"No, I mean we should walk there now. It's only fifteen minutes away."

This was the most ridiculous idea Yusuf had ever heard. "If I am caught without travel papers by police I could be deported, and for what? Candy?" How could the Israeli kid not know how dangerous it was for him?

"There are lots of Arabs in Jerusalem. Why would you stand out? Think you're special? And *I* am going for candy. *You* are the one who wants to see the place." Sam shrugged.

"You cannot walk," said Yusuf. How far could the Israeli kid get on crutches?

"What are you talking about?" Sam balanced on one crutch and waved the other around like a cricket bat.

"So we get out. So we go to the Old City. How would we get back into the hospital?"

"These will get us back in!" Sam held up his arm to show his hospital identification band.

"The nurses do bed checks." Yusuf's brain said, *Go back to bed, don't listen.*

"Unless you have blood pouring out of your ears they don't want to hear from you. You've been around here as long as I have. You know it too. Anyway, Alina and I have talked all night through a few times and nothing happened when they found out."

"This is not about candy. You want to do this because the nurse embarrassed you," said Yusuf.

Sam pressed his lips together so tightly they turned white. "Yes or no?" he uttered.

Yusuf hesitated. This was stupid. But to walk where Muhammad once walked, peace be upon Him, to tell Mazen and Yasser that he had defied the Israelis and broken their rules, to prove that he was not just a puppet to be bossed around—that was worth something. And to not lose face, to not allow someone to embarrass him, to protect his reputation—that was worth everything! Baba had said, "Be patient." Why should he be patient? And for how long? This was his land. They had no *right* to tell him where to go on his own land. How many other chances would he get? There were lots of reasons to go and only one reason not to. If he did not go, it would be because he was afraid of the Israelis, afraid of what they might do to him.

Yusuf took one deep, cooling breath, pushed the hospital identification band up his arm, and tucked it under his sleeve. *"Kol wahad wanasibu."*

"What does that mean?"

It meant that this was something he had to do, it meant that this was an important step, it meant . . .

"It means yes," he simply said. Yusuf stood very, very still. This was stupid, the stupidest thing he had ever done.

CHAPTER 7

❖

Run

How dare she call him spoiled? How dare she treat him like a stupid child? Swinging on his crutches, determined to get away from bossy nurses, overbearing parents, rules, and doctors, Sam pushed on. They could all go to hell.

No one stopped them. The soldiers in the parking lot ignored them too. In just moments, Sam and Yusuf were off hospital property.

A bus passed. "Run!" Sam swung the crutches forward and the two raced toward the stop half a block away.

The bus did not even pretend to slow down.

"Now what?" puffed Yusuf.

"We walk. It's downhill." Sam grimaced. Maybe this was not such a good idea. He glanced at Pirate Boy. Surely he would chicken out.

"We can cut through Issawiyya. It's faster. I have seen it on a map." Yusuf pointed to a sign.

Sam hesitated. Issawiyya was an Arab neighborhood within Jerusalem. The lucky residents there had Jerusalem identification cards and even all the social benefits that Israelis had, including health insurance. But Jews did not go in there, not alone, and never at night. Sam's chest tightened.

"What? You scared the big bad Arabs are going to eat you?" Yusuf crowed.

Sam looked back up the hill. The hospital lights did not beckon him to return; they taunted him.

Yusuf moved closer and looked Sam in the eye. "So, you believe the stories—that all Palestinians are just waiting to kill you." He was kidding, but every Palestinian knew that Israelis were fed a lot of propaganda by their own government.

The muscles in Sam's neck tensed and his fingers, crimped around his crutches, tightened. There was no real division between the land Arabs lived on and his land. All he had to do was move forward, and he was there.

"I'm not afraid of you or anyone. Are you sure this is the way?" asked Sam.

Yusuf nodded, but he might just as well have shaken his head. He was *almost* sure.

"Screw you." Sam's crutches moved forward almost on their own. He was not afraid, he was not afraid, he was not afraid. He was terrified.

Yusuf took the lead. He was feeling his way, step by step, his toes seeking out stones and anything else that might trip him up. He wanted to stretch out his arms, protect himself from banging into anything, but instead he kept them pinned to his side. Luckily the Israeli kid could not walk too fast.

Sam found it hard to catch his breath. The bright lights were behind them. Issawiyya was in *his* Israel, but now he felt like he was in Arab territory. The streetlights here were dimmer, the ground underfoot was rough, and the roads sloped. It was hard to keep up, but it was harder still to plant the rubber tips of his crutches on firm ground. Each time he stumbled, the crutches jacked up under his armpits.

He stopped for a moment. Pools of pale light from the streetlights illuminated piles of garbage. The roads were narrow, some too narrow for anything more than a cart. The stink of urine seared the inside of his nose. Great blocks and smaller chunks of cement were scattered about, some in front of doors, likely to prevent people from parking taxis and cars too close. Even in the moonlight he could tell that this was a desperate place. Nothing grew here. Issawiyya was an ugly scrub of land. How could this place be just a stone's throw from *his* Israel? Why did the Arabs want to stay in this awful place? This was just more proof of how stubborn they were. They could go to Jordan, Lebanon, or other Arab countries, like Syria. Why did they stay?

"Do not stop," ordered Yusuf. Sam carried on. Neither spoke.

On either side of the road, corrugated tin and chipped whitewashed stone surrounded the houses. The doors were wooden and old. Strands of light broke through crevices and holes. A child's wail rose up from behind a wall. Someone was shouting. A door slammed. The sounds mingled with wafts of garlic and spices. Without stopping, without focusing, Sam tried to peek into the homes. He caught glimpses of private gardens.

Yusuf stopped short. Sam banged into the back of him. "What's wrong?" he asked. Pirate Boy's shoulders were hunched.

"Get down." Yusuf grabbed Sam by the shirt and forced him to crouch behind a crumbling wall. He was listening to something. Then Sam heard it too. There were voices ahead, not yelling but laughter. Both pressed their backs against the wall and listened. Sam's bad leg was bent under him. The air seemed to pulse *danger*, *danger*, *danger*. He looked up at the stars. The feeling of terror was sudden. He had followed an almost blind kid into enemy territory! He didn't even know the guy.

"What is it?" Sam asked frantically.

"Maybe a gang, ahead." Yusuf spoke in short huffs.

Grabbing the lip of a wall, Sam hoisted himself up on wobbly legs and peeked over the top. All he could see were shadows. As his eyes focused, the shadows turned into the shapes of boys and young men. They were jostling, laughing, and nudging one another. Sam tried to take a deep breath but could not get air past his teeth. What had he done? Ten minutes ago he'd been safe. Visions popped into his head: his father reading in his chair, his mother talking to his sister, Judy, about her upcoming twelfth grade school trip to Auschwitz, Annah Weise and her scabby dog, soccer games, and piano lessons. He thought of Mr. Rosenthal. *Breathe, breathe.* His daughter was dead. Was he sitting shivah alone? *Breathe.* "Ima, Abba, sorry, sorry, sorry," he mumbled.

"Shut up." Yusuf nudged him. Sam glued his lips together. "Come on." Yusuf stood, poised to bolt.

Sam could not read Yusuf's face in the dark. "Come where?" he asked quietly. He could not outrun a bunch of Arab thugs. If they caught him, he'd be beaten to death, he was sure of it.

Sam slid back down and clasped his good leg to his chest, while the other stuck out like a pole. They heard a bolt slip its casing and a door squeak open. Sam covered his head with his arms as pinpricks of pain shot up his leg. His phone went off.

"Shut it off, shut it off!" In the dark, Yusuf panicked beyond reason.

Sam fumbled in his pocket. It was a little button, a tiny

thing on the top of the phone. *Stop, stop, stop.* He hit the switch just as shards of light fell on the ground between his feet.

"*Shoo hada?*" It was a woman's voice. There was a pause, and then he heard the crunch of gravel under her feet as she spun around. Sam could not bring himself to look up. And then, as if Jehovah Himself were reaching down from the heavens, Sam felt himself being lifted by the shirt. He cried from his gut as a hand clamped over his mouth. There was a scuffle.

"Shhh," she hissed through her teeth. She was strong. She twisted him around like washing on a line, then grabbed the back of his neck and shook him like a dog shakes a toy. Again, he heard the tortured squeak of a door before landing face first on cement tiles. His nose, forehead, and cheeks felt as if they had been scorched by fire. Moaning, he rolled over, instinctively covering his face with his hands. He looked up through the crux of his arms and saw intertwined olive branches above and glittering stars beyond. Walls surrounded him and then—*woof*—the air vacated his lungs. Yusuf had landed on top of him. In a burst of strength, Sam heaved Yusuf off with both hands. Yusuf rolled over, knocking his arms, head, and legs against a hard floor.

"*Shoo bidek min hel makan?*" The woman's voice was low and raspy. Sam and Yusuf, lying on the floor, stared up at her. She wore a plain dress and a simple headscarf. A small gas lamp glowed yellow but gave off very little light.

Yusuf answered the woman in Arabic. "*Mit asif ala el aza'a.*"

"What are you saying?" Sam whispered.

The woman's eyes widened at the sound of Sam's Hebrew. With hands riveted to her hips and a mouth pulled as tight as a pursestring, she stared hard at Sam, then spoke more Arabic. "What is she saying?" whispered Sam.

"She wants to know why I brought a Jew into this place."

"I want to know too."

"I told her that we are from the hospital. Everyone here knows about the hospital."

"You are stupid boys, do you hear?" She spoke in half-Arabic, half-Hebrew, while shaking a finger at Yusuf. She leaned down, grabbed Yusuf's arm, and shoved the sleeve of his sweater up. She peered down at his hospital bracelet. Pivoting on her heels she did the same to Sam.

"Go, sit and wait." She pointed inside the house.

Sit, wait—Sam got it. Where were his crutches? Yusuf held out his hand. "Get away!" Sam slapped back the offending hand and pulled himself up using an iron outdoor table. Feeling his way along the wall, he entered the house, then hopped across a marble floor and an intricate, multi-colored Persian rug, before flopping on a low sofa. The frame of the sofa was handcarved, the seat hard, the pillows lush. Yusuf, trailing behind, thumped down beside him.

"What's happening?" Sam whispered.

"Do not speak Hebrew," Yusuf advised.

Sam looked around without moving his head more than an inch in any direction. There were books on a bookshelf. Books? In an Arab home! High up on the shelf was a book covered with a red velvet cloth—the Qu'ran, he guessed.

Sam tried not to stare but everything was so different and yet so familiar! The room was spotless and painted in oranges, reds, and blues—mostly blues: cobalt blue, navy blue, sapphire blue, indigo, and cerulean, the blue of the Israeli flag. His eyes trailed from object to object. A large, round, brass table perched on dark wooden legs sat in the middle of the room. He recognized the brass brazier. He had seen charcoal-burning stoves before, in the Arab section of the Old City. There were painted vases in each of the four windows and handwoven baskets in the corners. Weeping vines and herbs tumbled out of them, some dusting the floor. He could smell jasmine, rosemary, and mint. The ceiling was very high and there was a large rattan fan tucked up in an arch.

Only then did Sam notice a fat, silent toddler with beady black eyes perched in a Fisher-Price high chair.

Drool dangled off the baby's chin and hung there like a dewdrop. As if to announce himself, the baby banged the tray of the chair with a tiny fist. The sound was like a gunshot. Sam felt faint.

The woman pulled back a heavy, gold-and-red woven curtain, revealing an arched, tiled hallway. She stormed down the little hall with purpose. Sam peered after her. She reached for a phone and began pacing back and forth while speaking quietly and urgently into it. He could see a fridge, a modern stove, and even a dishwasher. It was amazing. He had thought that Arabs lived like they did in olden times, that when they were not making bombs and thinking of ways to kill Israelis they cooked over open fires and washed their clothes in streams. The houses, streets, and public buildings all looked so dilapidated. He'd assumed that the insides looked the same. But this place was warm and inviting.

Sam twisted around. There was a small alcove, just an indentation in the wall, and tucked in there was a white folding chair. When he leaned forward he could also see a table made of blond wood, and then, most surprising of all, he saw an Apple computer. His mouth flapped open.

They sat. They waited. Time ticked by. Just when Sam thought he might make a run for it, the door burst open. Yusuf cowered, and Sam covered his chest with his arms. A man—a giant—filled the doorway. In one hand he held

Sam's crutches, and the other hand was balled into a fist.
He glared at the boys. He had the same dark eyes as the
baby—stone hard and fierce. He wore a baseball cap and a
black-and-white scarf around his neck. His beard was short
and trimmed.

"How have you come to this place?" He spoke in
Hebrew.

In a wobbly voice, coughing and sputtering, Yusuf
answered the man in Arabic, then showed him his hospital
bracelet. Sam shot a glance toward the woman. She must
have told the man that there was an Israeli in the house. The
baby protested against the sudden loud noise and let out
a wail.

The man turned, faced Sam, and spoke in Hebrew.
"Why have you come here to my small piece of land? Do
you think you can just walk anywhere you please?"

Sam lurched back as the hailstorm of words hurtled
toward him like bullets from a gun. Was he supposed to
answer? "We are going to the Old City."

The man looked from boy to boy. He was astonished.
"Then you are going the wrong way!" He turned his back
and mumbled something to the woman, who surely had to
be his wife. She was dressed differently now. A dark robe
covered her from head to foot and a black headscarf covered
all of her hair. She picked the baby up and jostled him on
her hip.

"Here!" The Arab dropped the crutches beside Sam and left, the door banging behind him. The woman and baby disappeared down a hallway, her robe billowing behind her like a black cloud. Emptied of sound, there was a kind of void in the room. Except there *was* a sound—the thin whistle of a kettle on the boil.

Sam bounced up and, hopping on one foot, reached for one crutch. "*The wrong way! We went the wrong way!*" he sputtered.

"I am sorry. Our maps, yours and mine, are different. Where are you going?" Yusuf folded his arms around his knees and rocked back and forth.

"I'm getting out of here." Sam swayed on his feet.

"And where will you go?" Yusuf muttered.

"I'm going through that door, up the hill, and back to civilization." Face flushed, huffing, Sam jammed one crutch under an armpit and, balancing precariously on one foot, reached down for the other crutch.

"He has gone to get a car to drive us out." Yusuf rested his head on his knees.

"And you trust him? What if she has called Hamas? What if he tells people that they've captured a Jew?" And then a thought; it was sudden and nearly brought him to his knees. Yusuf was one of them—a Palestinian, a Muslim. He'd had a teacher once who'd said, "Never trust them. They want to push us into the sea. They want us dead.

Do not let down your guard, do not give them an inch. If you do, you put us all in danger." Sam was about to be kidnapped, or worse.

"These people are being kind. They want to protect us." Yusuf clamped his hands over his face and his voice came from between his fingers.

"Kind? There are a bunch of boys outside who look like they could kill me just because I'm an Israeli. How is that kind?" Sam said.

"What would happen if a Palestinian kid was discovered walking around a settlement at night, or even in the day? What would the settlers do?"

"They wouldn't kill you," he said.

"Are you sure?" answered Yusuf.

The truth was, Sam really didn't know. Some of the settlers were violent, all had guns, and many had trained guard dogs.

"Why does this Arab want to protect me, an Israeli?"

"You think this is about you? It is not you who is in trouble, it is me." Yusuf's voice caught in his throat.

Sam stopped and stared. "You?"

"They will think that I am a collaborator, a traitor. To have a friend who is an Israeli isn't good in this place."

"What do they do to collaborators?" Sam leaned in to hear the answer.

"It is bad enough that I am in an Israeli hospital," said Yusuf.

Sam reared backward. It had never occurred to him . . . he had never imagined. Sam leaned down and whispered in Yusuf's ear, "Just tell them that we're not friends, that we hate each other."

"We are here together. Why would they believe such a thing?" Yusuf's voice broke.

"Then why did you insist we come here?" Sam was nearly speechless.

"I am not from here . . . I did not think it would be like this. I saw this route on the virtual tour of Jerusalem on the computer in the hospital. It looked safe. I thought it was a shortcut. And . . . I did not think you would come." He sounded defeated.

"But why? *Why?*" Sam slammed his crutch into the floor, then quickly peered up at the door. He hadn't meant to make so much noise.

Yusuf's face went dark. "Because everyone knows that Israelis would not even enter a Palestinian area to take a piss. And anyway, everyone knows Israelis are cowards."

The woman came down the little hall holding a tray filled with small dishes of food. Sam wavered on his crutches. *Cowards?*

"Sit, you are insulting our hosts," muttered Yusuf.

Host? He was not a guest.

"Sit!" Yusuf smacked the pillows beside him.

"Don't tell me what to do." Shoulders up, hands clenched in fists, Sam sat.

The tray was loaded with bread, olives, pickles, hummus; and tea in glass cups. Sam loved hummus, it was his favorite food. In the hospital, when his mother had put out his McDonald's hamburger, he had looked enviously at the food that Pirate Boy's mother had brought. He eyed the tea suspiciously. Arabs stored water in black barrels strapped to rooftops like saddlebags on camels. Likely, the water would make him sick.

The woman, his "hostess," placed the tray on the table and, with a graceful sweep of her arm, motioned to the food. Sam looked up into her face. She was not as old as he'd first thought. He just hadn't actually looked at her before. Helplessness overwhelmed him.

"*Shukran*," Sam said quietly. That was the word Alina had used. He sincerely hoped it meant "thank you" and not "you have the head of a duck."

Yusuf looked at him, eyebrows up, mouth open. Sam shrugged as he sipped the sweet tea. At that moment, being poisoned was the least of his worries.

CHAPTER 8

❖

Do Not Look Back

The Arab returned. He blew through the courtyard, swung open the door, and hovered over the two of them like a tornado about to land. He spoke to Yusuf in a low, guttural voice—all spit, stammer, and flailing arms. Sam looked from man to boy and back again, trying to figure out what was being said. The panicky feeling returned—maybe it had never left. He glanced over at Pirate Boy. He looked as if he was going to throw up too.

Enough! Sam scrambled up, rammed the crutches under his arms, and made himself look the Arab in the face. The man's eyes were cherry-black, and his cheekbones looked as though they were chiseled out of stone. He lifted his hand and held it above Sam's head like a hatchet. Instinct told Sam to duck, to weave, to dodge, but instead he stood still, closed his eyes, and waited for the blow. And then . . . laughter. A flutter of air blew around his neck. Sam opened his eyes and looked down. A black-and-white fringed scarf lay on his shoulders—a *keffiyeh*, the sort of square scarf that people always associated with Arabs. Even their politicians wore them, but Israelis? Never. It was crazy, but the scarf felt hot, as though it were actually burning his flesh. Sam put his weight on his left foot and reached up to rip it off his neck.

Then, out of nowhere, another voice, speaking in Hebrew. "The car—it is here."

Car? What car? Who said that? Sam's head spun around so fast it might have been on a spit.

The voice had come from the courtyard. The man motioned for them to follow, then walked through the door and out into the starlit enclosure.

"Come," Yusuf called over his shoulder.

Sam hesitated. The woman was staring at him. And then she did something totally unexpected. She smiled. It wasn't a wide smile, more like an encouraging look, accompanied by a nod of the head. He smiled back, then turned to follow Yusuf, his crutches making a hollow *tap, tap* against the ceramic tiles.

"Wait," the woman called out.

Hopping on one leg, Sam turned around. He expected the smile again. He expected another wave goodbye.

"It is your Passover soon. We know all about that because we have the DVD of the show *Horseman Without a Horse*."

Sam had heard about this show, all Israelis had heard about it. It was produced in Egypt, and it portrayed Jews as evil, scheming monsters. The Israeli government as well as the U.S. Congress had denounced it.

She went on. "I saw how the Jews kidnap Muslim children and use their blood for making your filthy matzo." She looked at him curiously.

What? What did she just say?

"Sam, come on," Yusuf called out.

Speechless, Sam stared at the woman, his mouth agape. What did she say?

"Sam!" This time Yusuf yelled.

The woman waved her hand at Sam as if to say, "Go, go." She flicked a switch and the courtyard was plunged into darkness. The far door was open to the street. A yellow streetlight lit up the opposite side of the road.

Sam's eyes adjusted to the light. There was a car pressed right up against the house. The back door of the car gaped open. He couldn't have escaped even if he'd wanted to.

The man pointed to the backseat. Sam crawled in first, dragging his crutches behind him. Yusuf sat beside him. The door slammed shut. The driver was hunched over the wheel, a cigarette tucked behind his ear and another clenched between his teeth. He did not turn around or speak. Sam caught his eyes in the mirror. He saw . . . hatred. *He could kill me if he wanted to.*

The man who had arranged all this sat beside the driver. The car lurched forward. Sam jerked his head from side to side. Wait! Wait! The car was going *down* a hill. The hospital was *up* the hill, behind them! His heart banged in his chest. *Pray, pray.* Prayers would not come. His mind went absolutely blank. The worst possible thing he could do was scream.

The car stopped so suddenly that Sam banged his head against the back of the seat in front of him.

"Go quickly and do not look back," the driver snarled at Yusuf in Arabic.

Sam did not need a translation. Yusuf flung open the door and tumbled out on the road. Sam threw his crutches out first, then fell out after them. The car was gone before they could stand up.

They stood in the dark on an empty sidewalk. A grassy traffic circle was dead ahead and there was a traffic light half a block beyond it. There was no time to get their bearings. Cars spun around and around in the dark, creating brilliant, blinding streams of white light. The headlights on the cars were magnified into huge, fuzzy balls.

Yusuf lurched forward as Sam stuck out his crutch. Yusuf tripped and hit the ground with a muffled thud. Gasping and dazed, he looked up at Sam. "Why did you do that?" He was more shocked than incredulous.

"That's for getting me into that mess," snarled Sam. Pent-up fear had turned into fury.

Yusuf leapt to his feet. "I told you, *you* were never in any danger." He clenched his fists as he peered at Sam.

"You don't know that." Sam gave him a shove with a flattened palm.

Yusuf threw a punch that caught Sam in the jaw. Sam lost his balance and fell backward, his crutches flying in opposite directions. Yusuf threw himself on top of Sam. They were even. The one who could barely see did not need to see; the one who could barely walk did not need to walk. They rolled on the grass, back and forth, back and forth, both trying to claw the life out of the other.

"You tried to kill me!" Grunting, Sam pushed a hand up against Yusuf's chin while landing the other in Yusuf's stomach. Sam had strong arms—a consequence of being in a wheelchair and on crutches for two months. But Yusuf, naturally agile and quick, blocked, rolled, swung, and pummeled Sam's chest.

"Kill you? No one tried to kill you."

"You Arabs think peace comes from the barrel of a gun." Sam blocked a hit.

"I call myself a Palestinian. *I am a Palestinian!*"

"And what do you call Israelis?" shouted Sam.

"Thieves!" Yusuf shouted back.

"Thieves? What did we steal? I was born here, that

means I am *sabra*. My mother was born here. She is *sabra*. My mother's people go back three thousand years. We are here and we will not leave." Sam pushed Yusuf onto the grass.

"Your people were here thousands of years ago. You left. My people never left." Yusuf rolled out of Sam's reach.

Blood dripped down Sam's face and into his mouth. "Shut up!" Coughing, Sam rolled back toward Yusuf and swiped at him with an open palm.

"You shut up!" With clenched teeth and fists, Yusuf stood up. He rubbed his face with his sleeve. The lights, the traffic, the honking—all the sounds and sights swirled and blended around him. He had to get back to the hospital. Which way? He spun around, first left, then right, then left. He stretched out his arms like a blind man and then stepped off the curb. Cars fishtailed and skidded into different lanes. Horns rose up into a cacophony of earsplitting sounds. Brakes squealed.

"What are you doing? Come back!" Sam screamed. Where were his crutches? A headlight flashed on one. He grabbed it. Where was the other one? He pounded the ground. Found it. With a gaping mouth, Sam tottered on the crutches while watching as Yusuf's head appeared and disappeared, bobbing and weaving, in the traffic. And then he disappeared entirely!

"*Yusuf!*" Sam tripped, caught himself, and took two long strides toward the curb. "*Yusuf!*"

Yusuf turned toward the sound of Sam's voice. His head was at a peculiar angle and his hands were outstretched as if he were trying to hold back the traffic with his fingers. He took a step back toward Sam.

Sam stood, mesmerized. *No, no, no. He's past the middle. He has to keep going.* "Yusuf, keep going. You've gone too far." Sam's voice rose in pitched fury above the traffic. Yusuf seemed frozen. *"Yusuf!"*

Sam stepped off the curb. Cars peeled around him. Drivers bellowed out their windows. Sam kept moving forward: one lane, two lanes, three lanes. And there it was, the ball rolling out into the street. He could hear Ari yelling. *Don't think about that. Don't think.*

"Yusuf, *move!*" Sam cried. He plunged forward. Vehicles swerved around him. He saw terrified faces through windshields. The lights were confusing. He put both crutches under one arm and reached Yusuf just as a car veered around them both. Sam's arm circled Yusuf's shoulder. Yusuf wrapped his arm around Sam's waist. Both dodged and weaved before stumbling onto the grassy median in the middle of the traffic circle.

"Why? Why did you come after me?" Huffing, puffing, coughing, Yusuf wiped his face with the back of his hand.

Shaking, muscles quivering, his heart thumping in his ears, Sam stared up at the stars. "I am not a coward."

CHAPTER 9

❖

Everyone Here Is Crazy

One moment passed, then another, before Sam rolled over on his side and tried to balance on his hands and knees. It was no use; he flopped back down. He undid the Arab scarf that was around his neck and mopped up the blood that was drying on his face. They lay side by side, faceup on the grass. The full moon and the stars were all but obliterated by the glare of the city lights. The grass had just been cut and had a sweet, earthy smell to it. The sounds of Ari's screaming kept ringing in Sam's ears, and the sight of the truck coming at him . . . he blinked. It was the first time he'd remembered anything about his accident.

Yusuf rolled over and slowly stood. "Here." He held out Sam's crutches.

Sam sat up and grabbed them. He couldn't stand up. There was nothing to grab on to.

Yusuf crouched down behind Sam and, hands wrapped around Sam's rib cage, lifted. "One, two . . ." In a swoop Sam was up on his feet. "Are you all right?" Yusuf asked.

"No, but thanks for asking," mumbled Sam. Was he supposed to say thank you? He'd rather chew glass. He looked down at the black-and-white scarf, bloodied and worse for the wear. What should he do with it?

A couple holding hands walked toward them. Sam shoved the black-and-white scarf under his shirt but the boy and girl didn't give Sam or Yusuf a second look; they were too busy looking at each other.

The boys stood on the grassy median and considered their next move.

"What should we do?" asked Yusuf.

"We can take that bus back to the hospital." Sam, still a little wobbly, pointed to a bus stop down the block and across the street. Any bus would do. A taxi would be better. He fingered the shekels in his pocket. He didn't think he had enough money for a taxi. Walk—he just needed to walk somewhere, anywhere. Sam set out toward the traffic lights a short distance away.

Yusuf walked behind him, scuffing his feet, shoulders hunched, head throbbing. His eye, or where his eye was supposed to be, was beginning to itch. They crossed at the lights, a good distance apart, as if they were strangers. The bus stop was dead ahead. Neither spoke while they waited.

A city bus wheezed to a stop. Sam lumbered up the steps, catching the tip of a crutch in the door. As he regained his balance he had a thought: What if he just paid for himself? He wasn't responsible for Pirate Boy. He could wander the streets of Jerusalem until he was picked up by the border police and shipped back to the West Bank.

Sam dithered. Yusuf was on the step behind him. The driver was a crusty guy with one fat eyebrow that ran like a furry bug across his forehead. He gave the bulge in Sam's shirt an odd look. Sam patted his stomach as if to say, "See, no bomb." He paid both fares. They sat apart, Sam on one side of the bus, Yusuf on the other.

Sam pulled out his phone. There was a text from Alina.

Are you still mad at me? I had an idea. Yusuf can apply for an escort—he is allowed out isn't he? Do you know the rules? We could all go to the Old City after Shabbat.

Sam pondered. What should he say?

Yusuf looked around, made sure Sam could not see, then reached into his pocket and pulled out his uncle's old, black glasses. He put them on, then pressed his face against the window. The Old City was up on a hill in plain view. By day, its walls were the color of creamy coffee, more cream than coffee, but at night great floodlights turned the walls green, red, blue—magical and oddly modern, but not in a bad way. Yusuf took in a deep breath and held it. Exhaustion lifted, the persistent headache gone, Yusuf felt the call that begged him to *come, come*. He hadn't come this far to quit now.

Yusuf stuffed the glasses back into his pocket and grabbed hold of a pole to steady himself. He had never been on a modern bus. How did one make it stop? When an old woman in front of him pushed a button and the bus crawled to a halt, Yusuf just followed her off.

Startled, Sam looked up. "Where are you going? Wait!" But Yusuf kept walking. He walked right off the bus. *"Wait!"* Sam shoved the phone back into his pocket and ran, as fast as his crutches would allow, toward the side door of the bus. The door slammed shut in front of him.

"Hey, let me off!" He banged the door with the tip of his crutch.

"A broch tzu dir!" bellowed the driver, cursing his annoying young passenger. He opened the door, not to be kind but because the light had changed to red. Sam stumbled off the bus.

"What are you doing?" Sam hollered. "Stop, it's a red light!" Yusuf stopped. Huffing, Sam caught up to him. "I thought we were going back to the hospital."

"You go back." As soon as the bus moved forward, Yusuf bolted across the street. How could he explain to the Israeli what it was like to be denied something all of one's life and then to suddenly, unexpectedly, have it within arm's reach?

"You're crazy, you know that?" Sam did his best to keep up. The crutches chafed his armpits and the bloodied scarf kept slipping out from under his shirt.

"It's the Middle East. Everyone here is crazy. Just go back to the hospital."

Yusuf slowed his pace and gazed around. He could see well enough; the tree-lined streets were bright with lights. Everything was so clean. The houses were beautiful, the trees were lush, the hedges were full, and flowers trailed and meandered along flower boxes. This Israel, this Jerusalem, was unreal to him. There were no cement blocks blocking roadways. Garbage was not left in corners. Yusuf stopped in his tracks. A giant, very old olive tree, lit by a streetlight, was planted in the median. Where would such a tree have come from? And just as he asked himself the question, he knew the answer.

Yusuf put on the ugly glasses. Never mind what he looked like; he wanted to see everything. Hordes of people brushed past him, all talking loudly. Everything was loud— cars, trucks, music blaring from cafés and restaurants. Was a wedding going on, or a religious celebration perhaps? Street after street was the same: men and women walking, heads bent together in conversation. Girls and boys walked together, often with their arms linked. Girls dressed in revealing clothes—bare legs, sleeveless tops, sweaters hung casually over their naked shoulders. Some wore skirts so short he could see their thighs. Occasionally he had seen such girls in the hospital, and he had watched Western television shows, but here, outside, in public, it was different. Were they not ashamed?

Yusuf stopped. Two men sat on a bench. At their feet, propped in a special seat with a great big handle, was a round-faced, pink, gurgling baby. The men leaned in to hear each other's words. One laughed as the other smiled. They were . . . He could hardly bring himself to say the word . . . He knew of such relationships. It was on the Internet.

"What's wrong?" asked Sam as he pulled the black-and-white Arab scarf out from under his shirt. It was itchy. Where to put it? There were no trash bins. Maybe he could just tuck it under a bush.

"Those men, I think they are . . ." Yusuf turned away, and quickly, before Sam could see, he put the glasses back into his pocket.

Sam looked at the two men and shrugged. "They're gay men with a baby, so what?" Sam looked around for a bush. They were all too exposed to streetlights.

"But they will be seen. The army will arrest them." Yusuf was confused.

"Arrest them for what?" Sam scrunched up the scarf and stuffed it into his pocket. That didn't work. It created a bulge.

"To love someone of the same sex is against Allah's law."

"Allah does not make the laws in Israel." Sam flipped the scarf around his neck and tucked it under his shirt. "Can you see it?" he asked.

Yusuf gave him a quick glance. "See what?"

"The scarf. Does it show?"

"What scarf?"

They passed an intersection. The YMCA, with its grand tower, was on their left. The regal King David Hotel was directly across the street. Yusuf looked past the big cars out front and into the hotel. A great chandelier hung from the ceiling and shimmered like the sun. They passed stores and crossed traffic. He was looking in all directions at once, except straight ahead. Whack! He hit a great big, life-sized *something*.

"What is it?" Yusuf reached out and touched it.

"It's a violin. How blind are you?"

Yusuf's eyebrows shot up. "Why make such a thing? What use does it have?" He looked up at the thing. It was huge!

Sam shrugged. "It's supposed to be art, I guess, but maybe it's more like a decoration."

Yusuf nodded. They had such a sculpture outside the entrance to the Aida refugee camp near Bethlehem. Palestinians who had been displaced by Israel lived there. The sculpture was a huge iron key, a symbol of loss. Many

Palestinian homes had decorative keys displayed. It was said that one day those keys would be used to enter the homes that had been stolen from the Palestinians. So the huge iron key had meaning, but what did a huge iron violin mean?

"Come on." Sam walked past the violin and into the outdoor mall. His shoulders and arms ached but his heart wasn't hammering in his chest anymore, and he didn't feel as if death was imminent. They might as well finish what they'd started. Wait until Alina found out. She would be blown away. Sam felt his phone in his pocket. He'd text her as soon as he had a chance to sit.

The night was hot but the open doors of the stores blew an air-conditioned breeze into the open-air mall. Canopies above the boys rocked gently on the air current. They walked side by side. With a gaping mouth, Yusuf craned his neck.

"Stop looking like this is the first time you've been in a shopping mall. You'll attract attention . . . or bugs," Sam said quietly.

Yusuf snapped his mouth shut but he couldn't stop staring. It was so bright! There were people everywhere, talking in groups, sitting on steps drinking coffee out of paper cups, looking into store windows, eating in pavement restaurants—there were even guitar players singing to the starry sky. He had never seen such color. It was in store windows, in restaurants, on people—pinks, yellows, flaming red! If he turned his head quickly from side to side it was almost like being inside a kaleidoscope. His brother Nasser had such a toy. *Nasser*. Yusuf shook his head as if to rid himself of these thoughts. Not now. He would think of his family later.

Yusuf touched his uncle's ugly glasses in his pocket, but really it was bright enough to see. Tall, clean windows displayed clothes, shoes, art. Yusuf tried to sound out the English names of the shops: Rolex, Tommy Hilfiger, MAC, H. Stern, Nike, Polo, Ralph Lauren, Nautica, bebe, Castro, Ronen Chen, and one set back from the rest—Steimatzky Books.

In the middle of the walkway an Orthodox Jew, draped in a prayer shawl and standing behind a tiny, makeshift table, was offering to wrap Tefillin on men's heads and arms. To Yusuf they just looked like little black boxes with long straps, but he understood that they were important for some religious reason. They had biblical verses inside, wasn't that it? He watched as a young soldier silently laid a leather strap on the inside of his bare arm, hand, and fingers.

"Quit staring," whispered Sam.

Yusuf nodded, but there was so much to look at. A young girl wearing a black headscarf, a black sweater, and a long, desert-colored skirt walked silently beside a sweaty, thin, stooped man pushing a baby carriage. In spite of the heat, he wore a knitted cap and a long, shiny, black wool coat. Curls bobbed around his ears, and a bunch of little children swirled around the baby carriage like a school of fish. How did he make his hair curl like that?

Sam, swinging on his crutches, was puffed up with pride. He was imagining what it would be like to see this place through Yusuf's eyes. Beautiful buildings, people eating and drinking coffee in cafés, people talking on their phones, smiles, laughter, music—this was what *normal* looked like. There had been nothing here before—nothing but sand and wind and camels. Jerusalem had once been an outpost, a backwater, and look at it now. Look what the Israelis had accomplished, and in only sixty years!

Yusuf shook his head. All of this . . . it was . . . too much. He felt dizzy. "You have all this and *still* you want more."

Sam drew in a sharp breath. "How dare—?" But something caught his eye. An Israel Border Policeman—here they called them *Magavnikim*—wearing a beret, dressed in dark fatigues, and carrying an assault gun, ambled toward them.

"Police," Sam hissed.

Yusuf tucked his chin into his shirt as his heart suddenly thumped in his chest. He peered into the window of a ladies' clothing shop. He could almost feel the hand of the policeman gripping his shoulder. He imagined it all: they would demand his papers. Everyone was supposed to carry identification in Israel. When he had none to offer, they would fling him against the window, throw him to the ground, pin his arms against his back, and speak frightening things into his ear. His brother Nasser had said that Israelis did horrible things to Palestinian boys in jail. Was it true? How was he to know what was true and what was false?

Sam rolled his head around and rubbed the back of his neck, all the while searching, searching. Soldiers, guards, police came in twos, everyone knew that. There! Sam spotted the second policeman up a few steps, leaning against a wall, sneaking a smoke. Sam looked back at Pirate Boy. He stood out like a clown at a funeral.

Yusuf, his heart still pounding, glanced over at Sam's reflection in the window. Sam looked pale—even his lips were tinged white. But what did an Israeli know about fear? What did he know about police or soldiers who came in the night and stomped down doors, humiliating fathers and big brothers and terrifying mothers and sisters? Israelis knew nothing about fear.

Sam watched as the second policeman caught up with the first. They put their heads together and laughed. If Sam reached out he could almost touch them.

Yusuf kept his eyes riveted to the mannequins in the store window. Small pieces of paper, delicately folded, were placed at their painted toes. What did the papers say? He squinted at the numbers until they came into focus. *Four hundred shekels for jeans!* He caught his breath. These jeans cost more than a Palestinian family would live on for two weeks. These Israelis were rich beyond anything he had ever imagined.

"Let's get out of here," Sam whispered. Yusuf nodded as he watched the reflection of the policemen casually sauntering away.

Sam pointed to pink, smooth, and shiny steps that led up to a great plaza before the entrance to the Old City. A thought crossed Sam's mind: If they were caught, would he get arrested too? Maybe there was a reason Pirate Boy was not allowed out of the hospital. Maybe he was a security risk. Would Sam be accused of being a *collaborator*? He should have thought of that earlier, he realized. He should have thought about a lot of things earlier.

CHAPTER 10

❖

To Jaffa Gate

They would go through the gate and into the Old City, get a map, go to the Dome of the Rock, find the candy store, get out, get into a taxi, and go back to the hospital. No, they should find the candy store *first* and then go to the Dome of the Rock. There would be a real stink with the taxi driver when Sam told him he didn't have enough money, but he could tell the driver to come back tomorrow. No, that wouldn't work. Maybe he could wake up Alina and see if she had any cash. Whatever happened, once Pirate Boy had seen the city, they were going back to the hospital.

"Jaffa Gate is up there." Sam motioned to the top of the stairs that rose up from the shopping area. The steps were like the ones he'd seen in pictures of the Roman Coliseum. The gate was the smallest of the open gates into the Old

City. It led to the city's Christian and Armenian quarters and, dead ahead, the Muslim quarter. Sam had never been through that gate—not that he went there much. The Old City was mostly for tourists.

Sam's pocket vibrated. Balancing on his crutches, he pulled out his phone and looked at the time: 10:00 p.m. Had anyone in the hospital noticed that they were missing?

"There's a text from Alina," he called out to Yusuf, who was a few steps ahead, still gawking at something.

Are you asleep? Do you want to meet in the PR?
Bring Yusuf.

"What does she say?" Yusuf called over his shoulder.
"She wants to know if we're asleep." Sam began his reply.

Do you have any money . . . ?

He looked up. "Hey!"
Yusuf was now taking the stairs two at a time. He bounded and leapt as if the months in hospital had never happened.

"Wait! Where are you going? I said, wait!" Would this guy ever just stop? Maybe he couldn't see very well but he sure could run. Sam jammed the phone back into his pocket and yelled, "I said, wait!"

Yusuf stopped on the top step, pulled out the ugly glasses, and gazed across a large, open plaza. Tourists by the dozen milled about, snapping pictures. A young, chubby guy was racing across the plaza carrying a huge bongo drum, two music stands, and a box filled with papers. As if that weren't enough, he had two guitars strapped to his back. His flaming red hair and beard were plastered to his sweaty head. Yusuf had heard about all the crazy people who flooded into the Old City.

To his right, from the height of the Old City, he had a panoramic view of the shiny, new Jerusalem, the secular Jerusalem of restaurants and shopping malls. To his left, near Jaffa Gate, stood a baker with a cart piled high with bagels—he wouldn't have looked out of place there a thousand years ago, Yusuf thought. The Jaffa Gate itself might once have been a secret entrance, a kind of portal to all the mysteries of the universe.

Sam could not keep up with Yusuf. He paused halfway up the steps. Tingles reverberated up his good leg while the other felt like wood. Slumped over, he sat down on a stair and ran his hands through his hair.

Yusuf rammed the ugly glasses back into his pocket and came bounding back down the stairs. "Here." He held out his hand.

"I don't need your help." Sam brushed him away. This was the second time Pirate Boy had tried to play Superman.

"You are taking too long." Yusuf put his hands on his hips and did his best to glare with one eye. It was difficult.

"Go away." Taking a deep breath, Sam stood and made the grueling climb, step by step, alone. It took a while, but he made it to the top.

Yusuf wandered across the plaza as Sam, in full view of the gate, thumped down on a stone bench. Now his butt hurt. His crutches clattered to the ground as he pulled his phone out of his pocket. There wasn't much power left. What should he say to Alina? It wasn't like he could tell her what he was up to.

I am running around Jerusalem with the One-Eyed Pirate who has no papers. Almost got kidnapped, perhaps poisoned (time will tell) by a Palestinian woman, driven in a car with two Hamas rejects, nearly got run over, just missed getting arrested, and now off to play the happy tour guide.

No, that would definitely not work. He pushed "Delete." He would just ask her if she had any money he could borrow.

Do you have . . .

"Let's go." Anxious, shifting his weight from foot to foot, Yusuf hovered over him.

"Go where? Do you even know where you're going? You could get lost and never be found, the Wandering Palestinian. Anyway, I just want to go to the candy place." Sam slipped his phone back into his pocket.

"Forget the candy shop. And do you know your way around the Old City?" Yusuf spun on his heels.

"Yes, of course." Sam pursed his lips.

"Okay, take me to Al-Aqsa." Yusuf glared at him again.

"What's that?" asked Sam.

"See? *You* are the idiot. Al-Aqsa is a huge mosque. Five thousand people can worship at the same time! It is where the Dome of the Rock is. That's where Prophet Muhammad, peace be upon Him, ascended to Heaven," said Yusuf.

"You mean where the First and Second Temples stood?" Sam wavered. He wasn't really sure about the religious stuff.

Ignoring him, Yusuf stormed across the plaza and stood at the entrance of Jaffa Gate. He touched the ancient wall. The rough stone felt cool under his fingers. They could be in any time in history but in only one place on Earth. Inside was the Al-Aqsa Mosque and the Dome of the Rock, its golden roof winking in the day and just as beguiling at night under the lights. *Come, come.* It beckoned to Yusuf with a crooked finger. It was too late in the day to visit the mosque but just to *look* at it, just to be *close* to it. He could feel the long thread of history wrap around him and gently tug him forward.

"Don't do anything stupid. They're back." Sam had come up from behind and was breathing into Yusuf's ear. Yusuf turned slightly and saw the same two policemen coming directly toward them. Their faces, once sullen and sunken, were now animated and on full alert. And then, they heard screaming.

CHAPTER 11

❖

Big Red

A bomb? An attack? Terror-stricken tourists and locals alike gathered their children and cowered. Others ran. The ones not frantically darting in all directions looked over to the screaming woman, most expecting to see a knife sticking out of her head.

"My purse, he stole my purse!" Arms waving, a camera bouncing off her chest, she pointed a shaky finger toward a figure that was quickly disappearing into the crowd.

"Come on!" Sam said urgently.

"What's happening?" Yusuf was looking everywhere at once.

"Who cares? Let's get out of here."

They ran to the steps that led back down into the relative peace of the shopping mall. Sam put the crutches under one arm and grasped the handrail with his free hand. He hopped down on one foot, step by step by step.

The pavement restaurants and shops were jam-packed. They lost sight of each other. Sam jumped on his good foot trying to see over the heads of the shoppers. Yusuf ducked and weaved, hoping to melt into the crowd. Sam spotted him halfway down the open mall.

"Yusuf," he half-hissed, half-whispered.

Pale and still, Yusuf faced a store window. He had no idea where to go. All he could do was wait.

"Come on. We need a taxi," Sam whispered into Yusuf's ear, then he carried on down the mall.

Yusuf shook his head as he fell into step. "No, no, we can hide and then go back to the Old City." He was so close.

"Are you nuts? We got lucky, really lucky." Sam, swinging on his crutches, slowed down to match the pace of the window-shoppers.

"We could go to another gate." Yusuf shortened his stride too.

Sam could not believe his ears. "The police were coming toward us. They have phones. Maybe they are looking for us—maybe the hospital called them. I don't know, but if they are, how hard would it be to find a kid on crutches running around with a pirate?" Sam reached deep into his pocket. "Wear this." He pulled out the crumpled polyester *kippah*. Yusuf reared back as if struck. "I will *never* wear such a thing." He shook his head so violently that he looked as if he was trying to shake a bee out of his ear.

"*They* know that too. That's why it will work. What about this?" Sam touched his neck, revealing the smallest piece of Palestinian scarf. "Now put it on." A spray of spit accompanied Sam's command.

Yusuf's lips, clamped tight, lost their color. He would never be forgiven for wearing a Jewish cap.

"Do you want to get out of here or get arrested?"

Yusuf hesitated, then slapped it on his head. A small silver clip attached to the *kippah* pricked his scalp. He mumbled a prayer asking Allah for forgiveness.

They walked on, this time ignoring the brilliantly lit stores and attractions. And then, right at the entrance to the mall and beside the giant violin, they saw the huge, sweaty, redheaded man with the guitars and bongo drum. He was struggling with a box of sheet music. A page flew out, curled, drifted, and landed on the ground in front of them. The tip of Sam's crutch landed squarely on the music sheet.

"*Assif,*" the big redheaded guy apologized as he dropped the box and fell to his knees.

"No, it's my fault," Sam replied.

The redheaded guy smiled at Sam. "Sorry, don't speak much Hebrew, not that I'm not trying." He spoke English with a Texas drawl.

Sam, trying to look casual, edged to one side as a line of tourists barged past. Yusuf pressed himself against the wall, eyes glued to his feet. They hadn't been spotted, but the police had to be moving in their direction.

"Need some help?" Sam tried to sound relaxed, laid-back, as though he had nothing better to do than talk to a sweaty stranger.

"My wheels are around the corner." The Texan's giant shoulders heaved up and down. He might have been laughing or having a heart attack; it was impossible to tell.

"My friend can carry your box." Sam gave Yusuf a nudge. "Help him," he whispered in Yusuf's ear.

Yusuf stared down at the box. "Why?" He kept looking over his shoulder.

"He's got a car. Just help." Sam was desperate. He was speaking Hebrew. The Texan could not understand . . . he hoped.

"Why do we need a car?" mumbled Yusuf.

"To get us away from here." The desperation in his voice was reaching a frantic pitch.

"I thought we were going to take a taxi." Yusuf looked back over his shoulder and into the mall.

"We will if we can find one. Just shut up and help."

"You shut up." Yusuf heaved the box onto his shoulder.

"Thanks, man. Got to say, back in the U.S. of A. everyone told me that the Israelis were kinda rude, but I find everyone here mighty friendly." As Big Red spoke, his *tallit*, his prayer shawl, kept falling off his shoulders. And twice he had to catch his *kippah* as it slid around his head like a fried egg in a pan.

Sam motioned with his head toward Yusuf. "My friend does not speak English, only Hebrew. We have to go."

"The car is parked illegally, and you know how they are about unattended cars around here." With the guitars on his back and the strings around the drum laced through his fingers, Big Red barged out of the mall. People pitched themselves out of his path. He was like Moses parting the Red Sea.

"Where are you headed?" Sam followed.

"Out to the 'burbs, Ma'ale Adumim, what the Arabs call a settlement. Before I came to Israel I thought settlements were a bunch of huts all clustered together, you know, like forts in the Ol' West. I knew these here settlements were in the Territories, the West Bank and all, but I didn't know how big they were. Israel is not exactly front page in Waco, Texas. Don't get me wrong. I know plenty. Population of Israel is 7.1 million, 20 percent of them are Arabs." He spoke proudly, like a kid giving a school report at the front of the classroom.

Sam shook his head. This guy was a human cartoon! "I have family in Ma'ale Adumim. Can we hitch a ride?" he asked.

Yusuf shifted the box. Had he heard right? Ma'ale Adumim? Yusuf might not have understood much English, but he knew that name. What was Sam getting him into now?

Big Red stood back and eyed Sam up and down. "Sure. Glad to return a favor."

"I'm not going to a settlement," Yusuf protested in Hebrew.

"It's a *suburb*, and I'm not going either." Sam grabbed the strings of a bongo drum and followed Big Red.

"What's a *suburb*?" Yusuf was confused.

"Ma'ale Adumim," Sam replied.

"Ma'ale Adumim is an illegal settlement on Palestinian land."

"Let's just get out of here." Sam looked over his shoulder. Just as Big Red said, the car, a Honda, was parked around the corner. The American pressed a button on his keychain and up popped the trunk.

"I mean no offence, but I gotta say, Israelis are some of the worst drivers I've seen in my life, and I've seen some." Big Red leaned into the trunk to drop the box. It was hard not to notice his huge butt. "Got a friend back in Texas, name's Ham. He took out three mailboxes, a lamppost, and the backside of a barn with his Ford Explorer. Good cars, Fords. Don't see many here. 'Course Ham walked away without a scratch. He's a menace on the road back home, but here he'd be just a regular ol' driver." Big Red laughed heartily as Yusuf dumped the box he was carrying into the trunk. Yusuf didn't understand a word except maybe "ham," which was pig. Sam and the American were Jewish. Jews didn't eat ham. Muslims didn't either. So why were they talking about pigs?

Sam looked up. Police! They were standing at the entrance to the outdoor mall, peering up and down the street. *Jeeeeeze*.

"In ya get, boys. It's not far. Nothing is far in this itty-bitty country." Big Red slid behind the wheel.

Sam threw his crutches into the backseat then hopped into the front. Yusuf shook his head.

"We'll get out a few blocks from here. Get in!" Sam snapped.

"What's your friend got his shorts in a knot about?" asked Big Red.

"He said that he likes your bum, I mean drum." Sam slumped down into the seat.

At that moment Yusuf saw the police gazing in the wrong direction. He scrambled into the backseat and sat, glum-faced, heart pounding. What now?

Big Red punched 88 FM on the radio. Out blasted some old American tune. The car, seemingly of its own will, leapt out into traffic like a Texas bull roaring out of the stockade—at least that's what Sam imagined given the circumstance.

"I'm here for a year and having a heck of a time with this Hebrew language. I hooked up with the wrong girl back home, a shiksa, and a Baptist to boot. I've been sent here to the Mothership to mend my ways. 'Course my parents weren't born in Texas, but you know what they say, they got there as fast as they could. Now I'm livin' with my uncle and his family of a hundred, last count. There could be more born by the time I get back. My uncle is all Orthodox. The man's tighter than bark on a tree. I'm making a bit of pocket money busking while I'm here, so at least it's not a complete waste of time. I'm fixin' to leave in three months. I mean no insult, you've got a great little country here, but it's not America, that's for dang sure." He grinned.

"Maybe we could get out at the corner." Sam clutched the strap that hung over the door. *Mothership? Baptist?*

"Do you know all of Israel could fit into Texas thirty-two times? Why, this place isn't big enough for a decent-sized ranch back home," Big Red hollered over the blaring radio. "Now, if you want to talk big, think Canada. Heard of it? It's a big bejeezely country that sits on top of America like a hat. Israel can fit into Canada four hundred and twenty-six times. Imagine that."

Big Red talked as he dodged and weaved through traffic. Yusuf tried to sit up straight in the backseat. His stomach did flip-flops.

"Now think about this here Iran. The Iranians keep

getting all heated up about Israel. Why, Israel can fit into Iran seventy-six times. Makes ya wonder why any country that big would even bother with this little place, now don't it? Live and let live, I say." He pulled the wheel sharply to the right. Yusuf slid across the backseat, knocking his head against the door.

"If you could just pull over . . ." Sam tried again.

"Here comes another one of those traffic circles. Gotta say, I still can't get the hang of them. Hold on." The car veered into the roundabout. They could hear at least two drivers, and maybe a few passengers, bellowing at Big Red. They were yelling in Hebrew. Big Red paid no attention.

A sign came up: MA'ALE ADUMIM, 7 KILOMETERS, and beyond it, on the same road, JERICHO. They missed the exit and kept going, around and around and around.

Yusuf floundered in the backseat. His hands became clammy and beads of sweat collected on his forehead.

"Getting on these things is darn hard but getting off is a mite tricky too." Big Red veered to the right. "Dang, missed the turnoff again."

"Sam, Sam!" Yusuf reached over the seat and patted Sam's head.

Sam brushed him away. "I was thinking that my friend and I could get off at the next light. It's kind of late to be visiting my family . . ." Sam's voice trailed off. The glove compartment at his knees had popped open. He sucked in a breath—a Jericho 941 all-steel semiautomatic pistol was in plain sight. Could Yusuf see it too? Sam looked over his shoulder. Yusuf was hanging on to the edge of the seat for dear life. Sam shut the glove compartment with his knee just as Big Red pulled out in front of a truck.

"Hold on, we're going around one more time." Big Red pulled the wheel sharply to the left. Sam closed his eyes.

"Now you take them Arabs that live here in Jerusalem," hollered Big Red. "After that Six-Day War, when all this territory became part of Israel, they got all their civil rights here, just like everyone else. They can even apply for full citizenship if they really want, and still they're always complaining! Heck, even the Arab *women* vote in Israel. You show me how many of them other Arab countries give women the vote! Hold on tight, we're getting off this merry-go-round, boys. Damn the torpedoes." Big Red pulled the wheel sharply to the right. Cars honked, brakes squealed. Sam hunched over and made ready for impact. Yusuf dropped to the floor. More yelling from other cars, and some screaming too.

"Highway number 1. There you go, boys. It's all straight driving from here," roared Big Red.

Jerusalem was now behind them. Big Red turned up the radio and bellowed along with Lady Gaga, who was singing "Just Dance." He was ruining the song. The thought of Alina in a white Lady Gaga wig popped into Sam's mind.

"Lookie here, one of those 'flying checkpoints.' Look sharp! We can say howdy to our boys and girls in the army that keep us safe."

Big Red slowed the car until it came to a rolling stop. Both boys sucked in air. Yusuf, feeling faint, pushed against the backseat as if trying to disappear right into the stuffing.

Big Red rolled down the window. "Evening, gents," he hollered, which might have been a fine greeting had the soldier been a male. "Sorry, ma'am."

The young Israeli soldier rested the nub of her assault rifle against the window frame. The other soldier stood back, his finger on the trigger.

"American!" Big Red thumped his barrel chest, and for a moment no one spoke.

The soldier stared Big Red in the eye. Her glare was like a threat. She gazed over at Sam. The black-and-white scarf, tucked under Sam's shirt, burned. The soldier glanced into the backseat. Yusuf, with the *kippah* still on his head, sat tucked up like a cooked shrimp.

"Just headin' home, temporary home." Big Red pointed to a road sign: MA'ALE ADUMIM, 4 KILOMETERS. "Hang on and I'll just get my passport. Not the best picture I have ever had taken, but you know how those passport photographers are—no teeth, no . . ." At the same time as he reached into a pocket for his passport, the soldier thumped the roof of the car with her fist and waved them on. Shrugging, Big Red stepped on the gas.

"Not the friendliest gal in town. It's mighty hard to figure out which side the army is on sometimes. Most of them don't like the settlers, I'm thinking. Why? Settlers are Jews too, even if they're living in the West Bank. Can't say much about their clothing style, if you know what I mean. You show me an American woman who would spend her life dressed in a long skirt, button-up shirt, and scarf. Some wear wigs! Well, it don't matter what soldiers think about the settlements anyhow. The government says the army has to protect us. How ya doing back there, kid?"

Big Red looked into his rearview mirror. Yusuf hung his head over the seat like a lovesick dog.

"Holy mackinaw, as green as a new tomato. Don't hurl in this car! It belongs to my uncle. Hang on, kid!" Big Red stepped on the gas, passing the sign that said MA'ALE ADUMIM, and swerved into a gas station. Gas pumps lined a cement island and beyond was a long structure made out of a giant steel shipping container with a desert-colored tent extending from the eaves out into the parking lot. It was as big as a good-sized trailer. Blinding white lights better suited to an airport beamed down from huge poles. Martians could have found the place.

Big Red slammed on the brakes. Yusuf, one hand over

his mouth, barreled into Sam's seat, fell back, hit his head, then tipped sideways.

"Out you get there, boy." Big Red had got out of the car and flung open the rear door. Hand over hand, Yusuf stumbled over the crutches, scrambled out of the car, then bolted across the nearly empty parking lot. As if diving into a swimming pool, he disappeared into scrub brush at the far end of the lot.

"That's what I call a close call!" Big Red laughed so hard his belly bobbed up and down.

Sighing, suddenly tired, Sam retrieved his battered crutches from the backseat. "I think we can make our own way from here. My friend could be sick again, and since it's your uncle's car . . ." Sam spoke over the sounds of Yusuf vomiting in the bushes.

"Now don't you be thinkin' a little puke puts me off. Come on, I'm thirsty." Waving his dustpan-sized hands, Big Red sauntered across the parking lot like he owned the place. Sam stopped to glance over at Yusuf, who was still headfirst in the bushes, his butt pointing to the moon, then hurried to catch up.

Most of the cars parked close to the structure bore green license plates, Palestinian plates. Sam looked up and down the highway. Surely there were buses that stopped at the gas station on their way to Jerusalem?

Big Red and Sam passed foreigners gaping at a flat tire. Maybe they were Christians; it was hard to tell. And there was an Israeli couple arguing beside a Fiat. They walked on, Sam's crutches tapping the asphalt.

Inside the tent, men, Arabs mostly, hunkered over small cups of coffee. An older Arab woman sat on a box behind a glass counter.

"Three." Big Red held up thick, stubby fingers while pointing to sodas in a far cooler. Wordlessly, her mouth crimped in a permanent frown, the woman stood three colas on the counter. Sam searched his pockets for his shekels.

"My treat." Big Red grinned.

Sam muttered, "Thanks," and then stuffed one cola bottle in each side pocket and walked out ahead of Big Red.

It happened on the way out.

Maybe it was the way Sam was walking, or maybe the thing had just worked itself up the back of his neck in the car, but either way, the fringe of the Palestinian scarf was now in full view.

"What the dang?" Big Red yanked the scarf so hard Sam pitched backward. "What are you playing at, boy? I may not be a homegrown Israeli but I sure as dang know what this is. You are no Jew. Who are you and what do you want?" He spun Sam around and hovered over him like a black summer storm. Big Red had grown to twice his size. His fat fingers circled Sam's throat. He lifted Sam up by the neck and slammed him against the car door. Sam dropped his crutches as the cola bottles clanked onto the ground and rolled across the pavement. "Think you could pass for one of us? Is that your game? You got a vomiting Jewish kid to be your beard?" Spittle flew out of Big Red's mouth. Sam gagged. "I don't care if you are a cripple, don't piss on my boots and tell me it's raining." Big Red pushed his face up against Sam's.

Sam couldn't speak. He couldn't breathe. He couldn't even shake his head. Big Red let go. Sam hit the ground like a rock. A guttural sound shot out of Sam's mouth.

Big Red stood over him. "Listen to me, you little twerp, my mother may want me to do this Israel thing but I'm an American, and Americans don't put up with twerps. I ain't getting into trouble with the Israeli cops over no pinhead like you. You're going to keep your piehole shut, got it? You are not going to tell anyone that I gave you a lift. Hear me?"

Sam lay on the pavement, curled up like a kitten. He could hardly breathe.

Big Red climbed back into the car and drove away.

Yusuf staggered out of the bushes and sat on a cement block. He spat twice. Uck! All he could taste was vomit. Somewhere in the distance he heard tires squeal. Gazing across the parking lot he tried to focus his one good eye.

He searched his pocket for the old, ugly glasses. Before he could put them on his face he spotted what looked like a lumpy bag in the distance. The lump squirmed.

"Sam!"

Forget the glasses. Yusuf raced across the parking lot and fell down beside Sam. "What's wrong?" He touched Sam's back. Sam turned over onto his knees and elbows and retched. "Are you carsick? Try to stand. You'll feel better when it's out."

"Not carsick," Sam gasped as he wobbled his head from side to side. If it had fallen off and rolled across the parking lot, he would not have cared.

"What, then?"

"The American, he thought . . ." Sam tried to draw in a breath.

"Here, here . . ." Yusuf held Sam up with one hand and picked up the crutches with the other. Sam placed his hand on Yusuf's shoulder and, wobbling, stood up as best he could. The scarf lay at their feet. In a swoop that nearly toppled him, Sam grabbed his crutches and the scarf. He put the scarf between his teeth as he swung on the crutches toward the outer regions of the parking lot.

"Where are you going?" Yusuf called out after him.

A cement block sat between the parking lot and the desert. Sam kicked it. Nothing. It didn't budge. He dropped his crutches, bent down, and, with all his might, shoved it.

He grunted like an old man getting out of a saggy chair. Still nothing.

"What are you trying to do?" Yusuf leaned down.

Tears leaked out of Sam's eyes. "Bury it." Sam held up the scarf between two pinched fingers.

Yusuf looked around. "Try this." He pointed to a large rock beside the cement block. Yusuf crouched low and pushed the rock until it stood up on its side. "Quick!" he grunted. Sam shoved the scarf under the rock. "Now, you hold it up," Yusuf groaned.

Sam fell on his knees. With both hands and more strength than he'd thought he had, Sam held the rock in place. Yusuf yanked the *kippah* off his head, put it on top of the scarf, and *woof*, the rock fell over the scarf and the *kippah*. For a moment both boys just sat back on their haunches.

"It looks like a tombstone," said Sam.

"Yeah." Nodding, Yusuf looked over at Sam. "What happened to you?"

"He thought I was an Arab." Sam took a breath.

"He thought . . . You?" Yusuf could not help himself. He smiled. It was thin, closemouthed, and a little smug, but a smile nevertheless.

"Shut up." Sam grimaced.

"You shut up." Yusuf laughed out loud. He fell back laughing. He lay flat out on the pavement, still laughing.

"Are you finished?" asked Sam.

"No." Sitting up, Yusuf reached into his pocket and pulled out the rumpled paper bag. "There are four caramels left. Want one?"

"It's about time." Grumbling, Sam popped the candy into his mouth.

"Time for what?"

"Nothing."

"Taste good?" asked Yusuf.

Sam shrugged. It was the best caramel he had ever had.

CHAPTER 12

❖

Bedouin Hospitality

And now what? thought Yusuf. There they were, perched together on a cement block at the edge of some parking lot in the middle of the night. "How are we going to get back to Jerusalem?" Reality had set in. What was he doing with an Israeli? Why had he followed him out of the hospital? He was an idiot and he was getting tired and he had a headache—the knife-in-the-head kind.

"It'll be all right." Sam spoke with some assurance, and took a swig of cola.

"That shows how ignorant you are. You are just like all Israelis. You make rules for other people. We have to live by them but you do not. Checkpoints can move—they can be anywhere. What do you Israelis call them? Flying checkpoints?"

119

"I meant that we will find a way. We could take a bus back to Jerusalem."

"Do you have enough money for a bus?"

"Sure," said Sam. He had no idea how much it would cost, but what was the point of saying otherwise?

"Where are we exactly?" asked Yusuf.

Sam pointed to a sign on the highway. "Dead Sea, twenty-eight kilometers. Feel like a swim?" It was a lame joke. Yusuf didn't laugh. "It's not that bad," said Sam. "We'll just have to call your father. He can get your papers from the hospital. Or we could call my father . . ." It was the last resort, the last possible resort. Sam pulled out his phone.

"No," Yusuf almost screamed. "Do not call. Not now. Not yet." Would his father come for him? *Could* his father come for him? He was not entirely sure. What he did know for certain was that he would be in very big trouble.

Sam nodded. Actually, he had no intention of calling anyone at that moment. He was just checking his messages. But what if he did call his father? What would Abba say? He would be furious, that was certain. Sam looked down at the phone in his hand. No new messages from Alina. To save what little battery power was left, he switched the phone off and tucked it deep into his pocket. He stood, leaned on his crutches, then flopped back down onto the cement block, moaning. His armpits felt like they were on fire. He moaned again.

"You sound like a girl," said Yusuf.

"You look like a girl. Ever thought about cutting your hair?" replied Sam.

"I will see if there is a bus back to Jerusalem." Yusuf screwed the top back on the bottle of soda and headed toward the tent, leaving Sam to breathe in the night air.

As Yusuf walked toward the lights, Sam took a long swig of his drink and looked around. Funny, the harder they tried to get back to the hospital, the farther away they seemed to get. But what was really funny, in an odd sort of way, was that this was the most excitement he had had since the accident . . . no, since *ever*.

Ten minutes later Yusuf came strolling across the parking lot as if he hadn't a care in the world. He even looked different, somehow.

"Give them to me." Yusuf reached for Sam's crutches and began wrapping wool around the armrests and securing it with string. That was it—Yusuf's sweater was now a vest. He had chopped off the arms! "My brother broke his ankle once and was on crutches for months. My mother used to wrap up the armrests with goat hide. I couldn't find a goat. Try them." Yusuf handed the crutches back.

Sam slipped them under his arms and leaned down. "Better, way better." He grinned.

Yusuf sat back on the block and gulped the rest of the cola. "There's a guy in there, he's a Bedouin." Yusuf pointed to the tent that was attached like an awning to the building. "He said that buses don't run along this road at night. He lives in a village close to Kalia Beach, on the Dead Sea. He can drive us as far as his home and we can sleep on his porch. There are buses that drop tourists off at the beach at dawn and then turn around and go straight back to Jerusalem. He'll take us there at first light." Yusuf seemed pleased with himself.

Sam said nothing at first. A Bedouin—great. Bedouins lived in filthy black tents on the roadside. They had dozens of dirty children and drank goat's milk—likely straight from the goat. "Why would he put us up for the night? We could be murderers, terrorists," he said at last. And then a thought: What if the Bedouin was a terrorist?

"You don't know anything about the people you share this land with, do you?" Yusuf gulped his cola.

"Yeah, I know some things. Like, the Bedouins welcome guests. I saw *Lawrence of Arabia*. Great movie, lots of sand. But look, I don't want to crawl into a bug-infested tent and sleep with goats. I'm tired. I'm hungry. I want a taxi." Sam peered into the dark.

"No Israeli taxis come out here at night, and no West Bank taxis are even allowed into Jerusalem. Do you not know anything? And this Bedouin, he is a sheik, educated in Portland, Oregon. That's what he told me. That is in America, right?"

Sam looked at Yusuf in total disbelief. "You lie. He lies." This wasn't possible.

"Come. Meet him." Yusuf collected both bottles and headed back across the lot.

Sam sat in the dark for a moment. He looked down the road. Nothing but darkness. He followed. The wool on the armrests did feel better.

The lights were directed against the tent walls, making everything look like an old-fashioned photograph. Arab men, sitting on long benches, rested their elbows on the long table. Most were smoking cigarettes and a few sucked on water pipes. There was an aroma of coffee and scented tobacco in the air. The smell was earthy and spicy. None of the men raised an eyebrow when the boys wandered in. What if they all knew that he was Jewish? Sam had that feeling again, like he couldn't breathe with both lungs.

"This is my friend . . ." Yusuf and Sam stood in front of a young man wearing a sports shirt and pressed, beige pants. The man was beardless with dark, intelligent eyes. "This is . . . my friend . . . Sami," said Yusuf.

Sami? Sam understood the Arabic introduction well enough but . . . Sami? Did he suppose the name would trick them into thinking he was an Arab? Anyway, Sam was a Hebrew name, not an Israeli name. It was his great-grandfather's name, the one who died in the camp in Europe. He looked at Yusuf, who kept his eye firmly fixed on the man.

"Sami, this is Abu-Ahmad," said Yusuf.

"*Fee 'endakum ghurfa,*" Sam (Sami) mumbled. Was that right? Had he pronounced it correctly?

"*Wa' alaykom assalam,*" responded Abu-Ahmad. His eyes darted around the tent. He stood up abruptly, said goodbye to his friends, and headed out to the parking lot. Wordlessly, the boys followed. Sam struggled to keep up.

An old, blue car with a West Bank green license plate was parked under the light. "Let me help," Abu-Ahmad said. He opened the car's back door, reached for Sam's crutches, and stood them up behind the driver's seat. Shocked, Sam looked up into the man's eyes. The Bedouin was speaking Hebrew. A voice called out from across the parking lot. Abu-Ahmad motioned *stay* with his hand and walked toward his friend, smiling. The two men talked and laughed, each slapping the other on the back.

"He knows that I'm an Israeli," Sam hissed into Yusuf's ear.

"That's because of what you said," Yusuf hissed right back.

"What do you mean? I just said what Luba said when she saw you in our hospital room. *Hello.*"

"I think she is studying Arabic out of a travel book. Get in." Yusuf stood aside.

"What did she say? What did I say?" Sam crawled into the backseat.

"You asked him for a room."

"Oh." And then, "Well, he is giving us a room. It *kind of* works."

"Not the way you said it. Just do us all a favor and don't try talking to a girl."

That seemed easy enough. Where would he meet a girl?

Sam fingered his phone. Should he call his father? What would he say? He didn't *feel* like he was in danger. All they had to do was get through the next few hours, get on a bus, and get back to the hospital before dawn. No one would know, and this nightmare would be forgotten, or at least never spoken of—ever.

Abu-Ahmad and his friend kissed each other twice on the cheeks and waved goodbye, and in a moment they were barreling back down the highway. The radio played Arabic tunes. No one spoke as they drove through the desert.

CHAPTER 13

✠

A Place with No Name

The village with no name was tucked in the valley between two hills. As the car plunged down into the gorge the headlights flashed on a little donkey tied to a post, an orange trash bin, and faded election posters plastered on walls. Tough little shrubs, skeletal trees—carob and fig— grew in the shadows. In Israel, trees were precious. Here, Sam thought, they looked unkempt and unloved. When he'd seen pictures of plants and trees in the West Bank and Gaza on the television or Internet he'd assumed that Arabs either knew nothing about caring for plants or they didn't care. Then again, he'd seen something on the news once about Israel having control over all the wells in the West Bank—and all the fresh water. Maybe there was not enough water for the trees?

They entered the village. Stucco walls surrounded tin-roofed houses so small they looked as if a child had built them out of blocks. The car pulled into a bumpy alley that trailed around the house.

"My wife will prepare food for you," said Abu-Ahmad as he climbed out of the car. Both boys protested. It was late. His wife would be sleeping. Abu-Ahmad raised a flat palm. "You must respect our traditions. Travelers must always be welcomed with tea and food."

Hesitantly, but not unwillingly, they trailed Abu-Ahmad up steep steps. Starlight lit the way. The air smelled of jasmine and lemons. Yusuf went first, and Sam followed, grabbing hold of a handrail and hopping up the uneven concrete stairs. The effort of climbing left him flushed and gasping for air. Yusuf could barely see. Sam could hardly walk.

"What is this place?" asked Sam.

They entered a small, enclosed porch. "It is his home," Yusuf answered under his breath.

His home, thought Sam? This wasn't a tent.

"I have four daughters, so you must understand if I ask you to sleep here. It is comfortable and the night is warm." Abu-Ahmad, standing in the porch, turned on a small battery-powered lantern and then disappeared into the house.

Astonished, Sam gazed around. Three low benches covered in red-and-gold carpets, and decorated with red-

and-black embroidered pillows, circled three sides of the porch. Earthenware pots filled with herbs sat on spindly tables at the foot of each bench. A brass table surrounded by four leather ottomans was in the middle, and a white portable fan stood in the corner. Above was a ceiling made of woven vines.

"This place is really nice," Sam said, more loudly than he'd intended.

Abu-Ahmad reappeared wearing a long, orange robe decorated with swirls of color. *He could be a genie*, thought Sam. That was it, he was caught in some magical Arabian play, *A Thousand and One Nights*—something like that. None of this seemed real.

A ripple of giggling pealed through the air. The boys turned toward the sound.

"Ah, my daughters have woken up. They are curious." Abu-Ahmad parted a curtain that covered a window above one of the benches. The lantern cast a glow over two girls. Sam's mouth gaped open.

"Do not ask her for a room," Yusuf mumbled. Sam nodded.

One was perhaps twelve years old, and the other looked to be more like Sam's age. Her eyes were chocolate brown and her skin was tinted pink, but then the light was pink, and so was the scarf that was draped over her hair.

Yusuf nudged Sam. "Close your mouth." Sam snapped his mouth shut.

"These are two of my daughters, Mariam and Maha. This one will go to Ben-Gurion University one day."

Abu-Ahmad, speaking in Hebrew, laughed as the older girl, Mariam, picked up the fringe of her scarf, covered her lower face, and blushed. "I will bring tea, Father," she said quietly in stilted Hebrew.

"As you hear, my daughter practices her Hebrew." Abu-Ahmad spoke like a proud father.

Again Yusuf protested. "Your kindness knows no bounds, but the time is late." He also spoke formally, as if he were reading the words from a book.

Abu-Ahmad shook his head and spoke in Hebrew, "Sit, please. Any guest in our home is the guest of Allah." The man disappeared into the house.

Sam looked back to the window. The two girls were gone. "Wouldn't guests of Allah be dead?" he whispered.

"Shut up." Yusuf mouthed the words.

Balancing on one leg, Sam lowered himself onto an ottoman, lost his balance, and nearly toppled onto the floor. Yusuf reached out to help. Sam glanced toward the curtain as he waved away Yusuf's hand. He didn't want to look helpless. The curtain didn't move.

"She's beautiful," whispered Sam.

Yusuf looked at Sam with horror. "She is a good Muslim girl. Do not even *think* of speaking to her."

"Why not? You spoke to Alina. She's a good *Jewish* girl." Sam was miffed.

"You don't know our customs." Yusuf shook his head.

"Her father's here. You're here. We're in her house. Her mother and sisters are here. I'm on crutches. So what do you think I'm going to do?"

"That is how stupid you are. In our culture, girls and women must be protected because they are held in great esteem."

"I'm not stupid, and women can take care of themselves. They're soldiers and doctors and teachers and police. They're equal to men."

"Be quiet. You will offend our host." Yusuf kept his eye on the curtain.

"Fine. Then you can't talk to Alina again." Sam folded his arms over his chest.

Turning around, Yusuf said, "You just said that women can take care of themselves."

"Shut up," snarled Sam.

"You—"

Abu-Ahmad reappeared with tea in thin glasses, coffee in tiny cups, and three round flat breads topped with pine nuts. He placed the tray on the round, brass table and passed out the cups.

Yusuf sipped his coffee, but Sam tossed it back like it was a handful of nuts. Coffee grounds caught in his teeth and stuck in his throat. He gagged. Yusuf rolled his eyes, but Abu-Ahmad only smiled as he passed Sam a glass of mint tea. For a fleeting moment Sam thought about the water quality . . . and then drank the tea anyway.

After sipping and eating, Abu-Ahmad gave them each a blanket and bade them good night. "I will come to you before dawn. The bus back to Jerusalem is a journey of only thirty minutes if you are not stopped by the border police, but there has been an attack in this area so security is very tight." Abu-Ahmad turned off the lamp. "Let us put the night in the hands of Allah. May you wake up in peace."

They removed their shoes. Sam did not want to look down at his foot, but he could feel that the Velcro closure on the protective boot was stretched to its limit. And it was beginning to smell bad. He pulled the boot off and turned his nose away from the odor.

Both boys lay on the couches. Stars winked through a roof made of wooden poles and grapevines. Yusuf pulled out his rumpled bag of candy.

"Sam, there are two caramels left. Want one?"

"Or we could leave them on the table for the girls."

"Sam, you will never see her again."

"Hey, how do you know? Anyway, her father said that she might go to Ben-Gurion University."

"Fine," said Yusuf. He placed the last two caramels on the brass table.

"Sam, I know Alina is your friend. I wouldn't do anything to dishonor her," Yusuf said.

"Yeah, I know. Anyway, cancer or no cancer, she'd make you the West Bank's first astronaut if you tried anything." Sam reached into his pocket, pulled out his phone, and pressed the power button.

"What do you mean, 'tried anything'? Why would I go to space?" asked Yusuf.

Only a sliver of battery power was left. "*Try* anything, you know. Oh, never mind." Sam pressed "Messages."

"Tell me, why did you really want to get out of the hospital? Did you really do all this because you wanted to be a hero and get Alina candy, or because you were mad at the nurse?" asked Yusuf.

Sam sat up, the phone clutched tightly in his hand. "Yusuf," he said, "there are forty-three messages."

CHAPTER 14

❖

The Truth Comes Out

Alina had sent a picture. It looked as though it had been taken on her phone from behind a hospital door. Ima's arm was around Yusuf's mother's shoulder. Yusuf's mother had her hands cupped over her eyes.

"Go to the last message," Yusuf said. The sight of his mother looking so upset made his heart hammer in his chest.

Where are you? They keep coming to my room to see if you have texted me. No one has called the police—yet. Your father, and Yusuf's father too, are in the hallway right outside my door whispering. They are really upset! WHERE ARE YOU?

"Tell her where we are, quick." The power bar was almost empty.

"It's just a village. I don't know the name."

Sam's own heart was racing. *Sorry, sorry, sorry.* "The beach, what's the name of the beach?" He was desperate.

"Kalia Beach, Dead Sea." Yusuf tried to keep his voice down as Sam texted the name to Alina. The power died just as Sam pushed "Send."

"Did it go through?" Yusuf draped himself over Sam's shoulder. Wide-eyed, they both peered down at the black screen.

"I don't know. I don't think so."

"What should we do?" asked Yusuf.

"We could ask Abu-Ahmad if we can use his mobile?" suggested Sam. Both boys glanced toward the darkened house. It was unthinkable to disturb the privacy of the home; even Sam knew that.

"He said that the beach was not far, over the next hill maybe. If Alina got the text someone will come. If she did not, we will catch the first bus back at sunrise. Either way, we should go." Yusuf slipped his feet into his shoes. He couldn't wait another second.

Sam slumped back. His leg felt numb and he was exhausted to the point of nausea. He reached for his shoe and almost keeled over in the process. Wordlessly, Yusuf bent down, held back the tongue of Sam's shoe, and slipped it on Sam's foot. He placed the protective boot around Sam's bad foot. It was so swollen he could barely Velcro the boot closed. "Come on." He helped Sam to his feet.

They stood on the moonlit road. From the depth of the valley the hill ahead loomed like Mount Olympus. The Dead Sea was a short walk away—but uphill! Sam looked down at his feet. His right foot pointed inward, as if he were pigeon-toed. He could hardly feel it, let alone control it. Despite the soft wool on the armrests of the crutches, Sam's armpits felt raw, his back ached, even his teeth hurt. What had Abu-Ahmad said about an attack nearby? If soldiers in armored vehicles saw two people on the road at night they likely wouldn't hesitate to shoot. Sam looked over his shoulder. With luck they would at least see the headlights or feel the vibrations of a jeep coming toward them.

Walking uphill on crutches was nearly impossible. Sam counted each step. Halfway up the hill he caught himself before falling face-first on the asphalt.

Yusuf, who had bolted ahead, backtracked. "We can rest," he suggested.

Sam nodded while swaying on the crutches. The full moon revealed a bald and vacant landscape dotted with patches of black and gray, like a sea of lava. Only rocks bloomed.

Sam stumbled toward a large boulder. His lungs burned as he leaned his crutches up against the rock and collapsed on the ground. His leg jutted out at a peculiar angle.

Yusuf sat too. He pulled his knees up to his chest. It was Yusuf who broke the silence.

"I was thinking about Alina."

Sam ran his hands through his hair. This was incredible. "*Now* you think of Alina?"

"Why not now? She has cancer, yes? How . . .?" It was hard to form the question. It was hard to even know what questions to ask. Muslim boys were not supposed to ask questions about girls, and *never* about Jewish girls.

"One day she was playing tennis, and the next she was diagnosed with cancer. You like her, don't you?"

Yusuf vehemently shook his head. "She is your . . ." He paused and thought of the names boys called girls on Western television shows. "She is your *girl*."

"My what? How long do you plan to live? Stop watching American TV. You call Alina that and she'll hand you your head on a platter."

"My head . . .?"

"Alina is not my girlfriend. She is a *friend*."

"Then why did you want to buy her candy? That is what boyfriends do, buy their girlfriends candy, no?" Yusuf was confused.

"Maybe a hundred years ago."

"But—?"

"Enough! Fine, I wanted to do something to impress her, *and* I was sick of being bossed around by nurses and doctors and my parents and everyone. Kill me," grumbled Sam.

"Kill you! Is that what you think I want to do? Kill you?" Yusuf's voice went straight up.

"I didn't mean literally kill me. It's an expression," Sam muttered.

"No, that is what all Israelis think. They think that all Palestinians want to kill Israelis."

"We have been through that."

"But you said that I cannot talk to her."

"Now you're going to get us both killed." This was all too ridiculous.

"I do not understand. Who is killing who?" Yusuf was truly confused.

"No one is killing anyone. And okay, maybe in the beginning I thought she was hot, but then we became friends. Anyway, Alina will decide who she wants to hang out with."

"I cannot marry her!" Yusuf fell back on his elbows.

"Marry her! Who said anything about marriage?" Now Sam's voice went squeaky.

Yusuf shook his head. He didn't understand. "All girls want to marry."

"Who told you that? Have you ever really talked to a girl?" Sam shook his head.

"I speak to my sisters."

"You are so naive. When we get back to the hospital, if we ever get back, just talk to Alina normally. Don't say anything stupid, and don't mention marriage."

"I do not know how to talk to a girl." The idea of a boy being the friend of a girl was strange, foreign, *Western*. Anyway, it had never even occurred to Yusuf before now.

"Forget that she's a girl. Talk to her like she's a person."

"But a girl is not a person. A girl is a girl," said Yusuf.

"Ha! You said that Israelis don't think Palestinians are people, and now you're saying that girls are not people!" Sam was positively smug.

Yusuf fell silent, and they sat for a while. "Does your eye hurt?" asked Sam.

"Which one? The one that I still have or the one that is gone?" It was Yusuf's turn to be smug.

"It's gone? Really gone?" Sam looked directly at Yusuf. He could make out his face well enough in the dark.

"Yeah, you want to see?"

"Yeah!" Did the eyelid still work? Did it go up and down and reveal a hole in his head? What was behind an eye?

Yusuf flipped up the eye-patch. Sam reared back, lifted his arm, and gasped. Moonlight revealed—an eye.

"What did you expect?" Yusuf smirked.

"Is it real?" Sam moved closer and peered into the eye.

"Real? How can it be real? It's a prosthetic made of silicone."

"But it looks like your other eye."

"They paint it to match. Here, I'll take it out and you can hold it."

"Noooooooooooo!" Sam flung himself backward.

"I'm kidding." Yusuf slapped his leg hard. "You are"— he thought for a moment—"so *naive*."

"Shut up," said Sam. "And why do you wear an eye-patch if you have a fake eye?"

"What are you, six? The patch is to keep the dust out until the infection goes away. It could have been worse. My brother . . ." Yusuf's voice dropped to a whisper.

Something had been bugging Sam for a while. If Yusuf had been shot in the head by a soldier like he'd said, wouldn't the bullet have gone into his brain?

"What did your brother do?" And then Sam understood. He bolted straight up. Yusuf had not been shot. He had been in an explosion. "He built a bomb, didn't he? You said you were in an accident. Did the bomb go off? Is that what happened? He is Hamas, isn't he? *Isn't he?*" Sam leaned forward, his face almost touching Yusuf's. He was a double fool. Not only had he started to trust Yusuf, but also he'd actually begun to like him. Never trust a Palestinian.

Yusuf leaned back as if pushed by a sharp wind. What had just happened? Why had Sam turned on him?

"Nasser did not kill anyone. And how could he be Hamas? Hamas are professionals. They do not want boys who know nothing about anything. You think that we are all terrorists. I go to school, same as you. I play soccer, same as you. I have friends, same as you. I want to go to university, same as you."

Words that had been stuck in Yusuf's throat since he'd come to the Israeli hospital came rolling out, and nothing could stop them. He had things that he wanted to say, jumbled thoughts, hundreds of them—angry thoughts.

"You people push us too far. Do you know how the border guards treat our people? Woman soldiers ask grandfathers, 'What is under your clothes?' and then they laugh. Why do you think that humiliating us protects you?" Yusuf's voice rose in disgust.

"The soldiers are there to protect us, not help you," Sam sputtered.

"Your checkpoints are stupid. Many Palestinians sneak into your cities to work. They cross the deserts. Do you think a suicide bomber cannot do the same?" Just moments ago Yusuf had been almost happy, and now this?

"You defend suicide bombers. You defend people who kill innocent people," Sam shouted.

"I am not *defending* suicide bombers, I am *explaining*. You listen but do not hear. If you were chased away from your home never to return, if you were boxed in by walls, if you had your wells destroyed, if tanks ran through your streets, or if you were told that you were not *a people*, what would you do?" How could Sam not know? He must know. He just didn't care.

Sam sat back. What was this about? "Do you think we want checkpoints? We have them to protect ourselves, to stop you people from blowing us up. And do you think your people are so good and kind? Do you know what that *nice* woman from Issawiyya said about my people? She said that we kill Arab children for their blood. Does that make sense to you? Well, does it?" Sam pushed his face up against Yusuf's.

"And how do your people talk about us? You tell the world that we are all terrorists," shouted Yusuf.

"You *are* all terrorists," Sam shouted back.

"If your people die because we fight back we are heartless murderers, but if your soldiers drop bombs from the sky and kill my people they are heroes," cried Yusuf.

"*Your people* and *your soldiers*—you sound like a stupid old man. Do you really think my people would tell children to throw rocks at tanks? That's what your heroic Hamas does, it uses children as fighters." Sam's words traveled on a wave of anger.

"In *all* countries, people who are oppressed fight for their liberty. All people fight—children, old people, students, everyone. You say that you want a safe place to live and then you make a place that is unsafe for everyone. What if you drive us from our land? Will you be safe then? And when the whole Arab world surrounds you, what then?" cried Yusuf.

"The whole Arab world already surrounds us. You think that if Israel was gone, just disappeared like it had never existed, all your problems would be solved?" Sam's voice rose up like a fierce wind. "If Hamas were in control, girls wouldn't go to school, they would wear *burkas* and be stoned in the streets if they didn't do what they were told." He clenched his fists.

"Oh, really? Do you know the future? Because now *you* are the one who sounds like a stupid old man. I'm sick of hearing it. The world has changed. Soon everyone will have Internet and mobile phones. Soon everyone will know Twitter and Facebook. We will be part of the world, we will progress, no one can stop us, and you cannot do anything about it. You do not belong here." Yusuf leaned forward, ready for attack.

"We were here at the beginning of time. We returned to claim what has always been ours. We didn't come to conquer. We came in peace. And *your people* started the wars: 1948 and 1967 and 1973—all started by Arabs! How peaceful is it to start *wars*?" Sam's voice cracked.

"You think I don't know my history! Israel launched the first attack against Egypt in 1967 because it was scared! Scared, scared, scared!"

"We are not scared of anyone!" screamed Sam.

"You have been taking our land for more than a century. Even today, the settlements in the West Bank keep growing bigger and bigger, and on *our* land."

Enough! Sam gave Yusuf a hard shove. "If you stopped trying to kill us, we would stop taking your land."

Yusuf shoved him back. "Ha! You admit it! You never came to our land with the intent of becoming neighbors. You don't even want to speak our language. Why? Because you do not want to talk to us, to know us. You think you are brave. You are not brave. You are cowards."

Sam shoved Yusuf so hard that he toppled over into the sand. Scrambling up, Yusuf came back at Sam with a vengeance.

"Look at our army. Israel was attacked on all sides in the Six-Day War—Jordan, Egypt, Syria—and we won. We beat them all," cried Sam. He blocked a hit and pushed back, hard.

"You won the war but you did not win peace. You say, 'Look at the beautiful country we have built. We have pretty stores, big buildings. We have democracy. We have rights,' and then you take away *our* rights." Yusuf swung, and his fist made contact with Sam's cheek.

"If you hate us so much, why would you come to an Israeli hospital?" Sam shoved back. His nose began to pour blood again. He mopped it up with his sleeve. Panting, down on hands and knees, both boys squared off. What was happening? Why were they yelling? But neither could stop. It felt good to yell. It felt great!

"In the name of Allah I swear, my father was once a hero to our people, and now they call him a collaborator. My father no longer has a job, my sisters are shunned by their friends, my mother does not want to leave the house—all because I'm in an Israeli hospital. Do you think it is simple being a Palestinian? You want to know if we love life? Do you not see us fight with all we have, down to sticks and stones? We are desperate, we are t-t-tired, and still we f-f-fight," Yusuf stuttered.

"You're liars. Your teachers tell you lies about us. They say that the Holocaust never happened. I have read what your people say. They say that we made it up, and then they say that only fifty thousand died and not six million. Which is it? Did the Holocaust happen or not?" Sam cried.

"What has your Holocaust to do with us? We did not lock you up in ghettos, we did not push people into ovens. Why do we have to pay for the crimes of Germany?" Yusuf screamed.

"How do you know about the ovens if you say that the Holocaust didn't happen?" Sam, eyes wide, sat back on his haunches. He was more astonished than angry.

"Of course it happened. I read about it on the Internet." Yusuf also sat back.

"Then—then why do your people say that it didn't happen?" Sam stammered. He was nearly speechless.

"Some do believe that the Holocaust was made up, but most deny it because everyone knows that it makes Israelis crazy," cried Yusuf.

Sam took in a long, slow breath. "It works." He slumped.

Yusuf seemed to lose his breath too. "I know that Jews were murdered," he said at last. "I know that they were surrounded by walls in ghettos, but now you build walls that surround us."

"I didn't build anything," Sam said. "Anyway, they aren't walls, they are *security barriers* meant to keep us safe. And don't you dare compare us to the Nazis." He could barely get the words out.

"How can something as tall as a three-story building and made of concrete not be a wall? This freedom, this democracy, is only for you. You break your own laws. You have robbed us of our past. I have seen what happens to the olive trees your people take from our land. They are our trees that have fed our people for generations, and you use them to decorate your streets!" Yusuf crawled up and stood on his feet, angry once more.

"The land, *ha'aretz*, is our land. The State of Israel is our land, *Eretz Yisrael*." Struggling, Sam stood unsteadily. "It's not yours. You lost your land," he yelled.

"Land is not a hat. It is not a shirt. It cannot be lost and not found. It is here! You have built your country on our land." Yusuf scooped up sand and threw it in Sam's face.

Flustered, eyes burning, hands waving, Sam yelled, "There are one hundred and ninety-five countries in this world—Christian countries, Muslim countries, secular countries, and one Jewish country—*one*! We have a right to our own homeland. *Lekh le'azazel*!"

He laid his palms squarely on Yusuf's chest and pushed. Yusuf stumbled back, then lunged forward, grabbing Sam's shirt. Sam swung. The punch hit Yusuf in the shoulder.

"You're hiding something. You were in an explosion. You were building bombs." Sam was screaming.

"Do you think the Israeli hospital would have taken me in if I was building a bomb? I was not in any explosion. I was trying to stop my brother from throwing a rock at an Israeli convoy and I got hit in the head by a potato."

Sam wavered. He stopped. He tilted his head like Annah Weise's pissy, scabby dog.

"Well, say something," muttered Yusuf.

"A what?" Sam's voice climbed several octaves.

"Do I have to repeat it? I got hit in the head with a potato. It came out of the tailpipe of a car like a bullet."

Potato? Tailpipe? Sam staggered backward. "How?" he asked.

"We, my friends and I, stuffed it into the tailpipe and, well . . ." Yusuf's voice trailed away.

Sam looked out into the night, over the gray desert and up to the moonlit sky. It was like an eruption that began in the belly, a bubble that became a cloudburst that turned into peals of laughter, the kind of laughter that takes over the body and leaves a person gasping for air. Leg or no leg, Sam crumpled back onto the ground. He wrapped his arms around his stomach and rocked like an old man in a chair.

"A potato?" Sam tried to take a breath.

"Are you finished?" Yusuf folded his arms.

"No." And Sam started laughing all over again.

CHAPTER 15

Murder Is Murder

They kept walking, always uphill. But now the Dead Sea seemed close enough to reach.

"I just had a thought," Sam huffed.

"No . . . thinking . . . just . . . walking." Yusuf could barely get the words out.

"Yeah, but . . . potatoes have *eyes* . . . and . . . a potato took out your eye . . . I mean"—Sam took a deep breath—"that's pretty funny . . . right?"

"Very funny."

"Hey, you could be Mr. Potato Head!"

"What's that?"

"It's a toy."

"Shut up."

"From now on, every time I eat potatoes, I'll think of

you. Latkes, mashed potatoes, stuffed potatoes, knishes, kugel, baked potatoes, fries, *chips*!"

"I hope you get fat eating potatoes."

"You *Palestinians* have no . . . appreciation . . . for . . . irony . . . Listen." Sam stopped short. His shoulders snapped back. He took in a breath and waited. There! He could feel the faint vibration.

Yusuf recognized the sound too. "A patrol! *Go!*" Yusuf planted a hand on Sam's back and pushed. A great *oomph* jumped out of his throat as Sam pitched forward and rolled into the ditch. Yusuf jumped over Sam and flattened himself on the ground.

The ditch was much too shallow to hide in completely.

"Yusuf, my crutch," Sam whispered. The crutch lay on the road like a beacon. The rumble coming from over the hill was getting louder.

Groaning, Yusuf leapt over Sam, grabbed the crutch, and flipped it into the ditch. Crab-like, he crawled back, landed on a protruding rock, let out a small, muffled groan, and lay there miserably.

Neither moved. The jeep roared past.

"They will be back in a minute," whispered Yusuf. Sam's head bobbed in the dirt. Likely the patrol would go to the Dead Sea, turn around, and come back along this same road. "How come there's a patrol on this road?"

"Didn't Abu-Ahmad say something about an attack nearby?" Sam whispered. They waited, lying side by side, until the taillights of the jeep disappeared over the hill.

Slowly, Sam sat up.

Yusuf sat up too and dusted himself off. "Soon the borders will be patrolled by robots."

"How do you know that?" Sam asked, although he was pretty sure of the answer.

"Internet," said Yusuf.

Sam nodded. "Yeah."

Sam peered down the road and saw a flash of light cresting the hill. "Get down, they're coming back." The rumble grew into a roar that came closer and closer, and then stopped beside them. If the jeep had veered off the road, even a little bit, they would have been run over.

"I saw something." It was the voice of a young, male soldier. A huge spotlight, as piercing as a shard of glass, blazed out over their heads. And then, a flicking sound.

"When did you start smoking? Put that out." The second voice was lower and sounded older.

"Is that an order from my superior officer, Commander?" The first voice was light, jovial almost.

"Call it a request. Pass me the night-goggles and shine the light toward that ridge."

Motionless, the boys lay beside the jeep's tires.

"Why spend Shabbat in Jerusalem? Nothing is open. Come to Tel Aviv. I'll take you to a great club on Dizengoff Street." It was the older, more commanding voice that was speaking.

"I thought that street was dead," said the first, and younger, voice.

"What's old is new . . . I don't see anything. Point the light out toward the hills."

"I'll come if you introduce me to your sister," replied the young soldier.

"My sister would eat you alive. Look, over there," said the commander.

"I see something."

Silence, and then, "It's a goat. Feel like a kebab?"

The commander had a deep, throaty laugh. Then a mobile phone rang. "Speak," the commander barked into it. There were a few inaudible words and then, "Let's get out of here. And get rid of that thing. My father was a smoker. He died of lung cancer. Until his dying breath he acted like he'd never heard that smoking caused cancer."

Sam was facedown but Yusuf caught a glimmer of the cigarette butt sailing through the air. It almost landed in Sam's hair. Seconds passed and neither moved. They just lay there, still as death. And then the engine revved up and the jeep pulled away.

Yusuf smacked Sam in the head. "Agh! Burning hair stinks," he said as he took a deep breath. There was no getting used to fear.

Sam rolled over, sat up, and rubbed his head. Perfect, he'd almost been set on fire. What was next, a plague?

Something moved in the dark, a shadow—*something*. Sam looked past Yusuf and into the desert beyond.

"*Snake!*" he screamed.

"*Snake?*" cried Yusuf.

"*Snake!*" Sam yanked Yusuf toward him and, with herculean strength, hurled him over his shoulder. *Thud*— the sound of a sack dropped from a great height. Yusuf landed on the road.

"Run!" Sam was screaming, the effort tearing his throat.

Run? He could barely see! Yusuf scrambled across the asphalt and pulled himself up onto the rock on the opposite side of the road. Blinking, he raised his dusty face and stared past Sam. He stifled a cry as he put his hand in his pocket. Where? Where? Got them! Yusuf slapped the ugly glasses on his face. And there, shimmering in the moonlight, poised in the air, was a flat, broad-headed, thick-necked snake. The snake grew taller and taller until it loomed over Sam. It hissed, its forked tongue flicking madly in the moonlight.

Yusuf watched as Sam picked up a crutch and swung it madly. Again and again, Sam swung the crutch like a wild man. The crutch made contact and then slipped from his hands and sailed silently off into the night. The snake melted into the ground and seemed to disappear.

"Run, run!" Sam cried. Sam was trying to balance on one leg. Both legs crumpled under him.

Yusuf scrambled back across the road. "Hold on." He hunched behind Sam, circled his arms around Sam's waist, and dragged him across the asphalt. The two collapsed on the other side of the road.

"What was it?" Sweat careened down Sam's face.

"Persian . . . horned . . . viper." Yusuf flopped back on his butt.

"Poisonous?" asked Sam.

"Yeah." Yusuf ran his fingers through his hair. He felt sick.

Sam shuddered. Some people were afraid of spiders or rodents, but he hated snakes. All snakes. "Do they come after people?"

"No, we must have stumbled on its nest. They hide from people."

"He didn't hide very well," said Sam.

"We need to get out of here. Can you stand?" asked Yusuf.

Sam rammed his remaining crutch into the ground, pulled himself up, and balanced as best he could. "No."

Rocking on his feet, Yusuf reached out. "Give me your belt."

Startled for a moment, Sam pulled the belt out of his pant loops.

Using Sam's belt, Yusuf bound their two upper thighs together. Next, he took off his own belt and tied their legs together just below the knee. "Does this hurt?" asked Yusuf. He could feel the swelling of Sam's leg. It *had* to hurt.

Sam shook his head. His leg had gone numb ages ago.

Hip to hip, arms around each other, they took a step and stumbled. "Try again." Sam was breathing hard. This had to work. Maybe snakes were shy creatures, maybe they didn't attack, but he wasn't about to sit around and find out.

It didn't work. They staggered a bit, tripped, straightened up, and tried again. This time they fell, Sam scraping the palms of his hands on the road's surface.

"Wait." Yusuf pulled the laces out of his shoes and tied their belt loops together. Now they were attached at the waist too. "Count out the steps," he ordered. "One, two, three, okay, go." They limped to the crest of the hill.

They walked, arms across each other's shoulders, one step, two steps, on and on. Their hearts beat in tandem. Sweat dripped down into their eyes but still they kept going.

"What's . . . on . . . your . . . face?" Sam was panting.

"Uncle's . . . glasses." Yusuf drew in deep breaths. He was carrying most of Sam's weight.

"You . . . look like you're . . . wearing . . . two windows. I can call you ol' three eyes." He gulped back air.

"I do not . . . understand." Walking down the hill was proving as hard as walking up.

"People who . . . wear glasses . . . called *four eyes*." Sam sucked back air like he was suffocating.

"Why?"

"Because . . . never mind." Sam didn't have the breath to explain. "What happened . . . to your brother?"

"He is at home . . . high . . . unemployment. My parents say . . . he'll stay . . . in school." Both stopped and drew in deep breaths. For a moment it was enough just to stand and breathe. To their right, cloaked in darkness, was Qumran, the place where the Dead Sea Scrolls—the oldest surviving copies of the writings of the Hebrew Bible—had been accidentally discovered. Ahead was the lowest point on Earth, the Dead Sea.

"Come on. It's not far now," said Yusuf.

Sam gathered his energy to start again, but a question was holding him back. "I have to know, suicide bombing, do you think . . . Is it right?" Sam's heart pounded as hard as it had when Yusuf was almost killed in traffic, when Big Red pinned him against the car, when the snake almost poisoned them. A word pulsed in his ears: *please, please, please.*

"Murder is murder," said Yusuf.

Sam nodded. It was that simple. They carried on.

CHAPTER 16

✦

Kalia Beach

They stood on the beach. Yusuf undid the ties and belts that bound them together and softened the sand by scuffing it with the tip of his shoe. But it didn't matter whether it was soft or hard, both sank into the sand as if it were a feather bed.

Sam peered over at Yusuf. It was dark, the moon had set, but he could still make out Yusuf's profile. If Yusuf were not a Palestinian, Sam thought, maybe they could be friends, real friends—the kind of friends that have each other's back, the kind of friends who don't care if a guy has both legs.

"Does your eye hurt?" Sam asked.

"It is fine," Yusuf replied. What was the point of complaining?

Sam pulled off his shoe and the protective boot on his right foot. A sour smell wafted up. It was enough to turn his stomach.

"Need help?" asked Yusuf.

Sam mumbled, "No," and flopped back onto the sand.

For a long while they just lay there, side by side. There was no wind to create lapping waves, no fish in the sea to stir the water, and no early-morning birds to herald the dawn. Behind them were silent dunes, a mute desert, and stoic hills of sand and rock. Great-Aunt Esther's words floated back, "Never forget, Samuel, this land has belonged to us since the beginning of time and will be ours to the end of time." He belonged here. And if not here, where? If Israel ceased to exist, who would take him in? The world had turned its back on Jews before; it could happen again. Sam felt a sudden rush of tears. He swallowed hard. This was his land too.

"I was wrong." Yusuf's words seem to float toward him in the dark.

"About what?" asked Sam.

"You are not a coward." Yusuf spoke matter-of-factly.

"I shouldn't have made you leave the hospital." Sam's eyes were heavy. He felt weary, so tired it felt as if his bones were made of rubber.

"You did not make me do anything I did not want to do." Yusuf was adamant.

"In the hospital I watched your father," said Sam. "He stands like a fighter. He has the eyes of a fighter—like my father, and my grandfather too. My grandfather was the only member of his whole family to survive the Holocaust. When he was fourteen he came to Israel. He worked, saved, and got married. When my father was fifteen, his sister was born."

Sam paused. He had never talked about his aunt's death, not really. People asked him about it, grief counselors at school, mostly. He wouldn't talk.

"I think my father loved her more than anyone. She was out celebrating her acceptance into medical school. I was only eight but I remember. They were in a lineup to go into a club. Her friend went to the toilet. Lots of people were killed in that attack. I looked it up on the Internet. I think about him—the suicide bomber. I wonder if he saw her. I think of my aunt and what it's like to die in an explosion. Sometimes, after an explosion, I see ZAKA drive through the streets on their motorcycles. They're the volunteers who rush in after a disaster to help rescue the survivors and to . . . to clean up. They collect body parts, they even climb poles to scrape off splattered blood. My aunt's friend called our house right after the blast. I could hear her screaming at the other end of the telephone clear across the room. My father fell down on the floor. I thought he was having a heart attack. He was in the army at the time." Sam looked up into the sky. Sunrise was two, possibly fewer, hours away. The sky was purple, the color of the bruises on his leg.

"But you said that your father is a teacher, a professor."

"Now he teaches in the university, but before . . ." Sam took a breath. "He was a brigadier general in the IDF, Israel Defense Force. He retired last year."

Yusuf said nothing for a minute. Sam waited.

"Then he bombed *us*," said Yusuf.

"Maybe," said Sam.

"That's why you kept saying that I would get back into the hospital—because you knew that you could call your father and he would fix things."

"Yeah. Aren't you going to yell at me or something?" asked Sam.

Yusuf shook his head.

"You said your father went to university. Where?" Sam asked.

"In Oxford, England. Then he went to work in America in a place called Clarkston, Georgia. He worked in a McDonald's restaurant. When he came home he got arrested and was put in an Israeli jail for two years."

A minute passed before Sam said, "Why was he arrested?" The sky was black.

"For protesting," said Yusuf. "They called it 'administrative detention.' The Israelis said my father was a suspicious person. He was never charged, I don't think. Then one day he came home. *Kol wahad wanasibu*."

"You said that once before. What does it mean?" asked Sam. "Look!" Sam, suddenly wide awake, cried out. "What was that?" A streak of light crossed the sky. Was it a shooting star? A meteor? Cosmic junk? Maybe the space station. Sam scanned the sky for more anomalies. There was nothing. Had he imagined it?

Yusuf could only peer blindly into the night sky and wonder what Sam had seen that could be so exciting. They lay there in silence again.

"Yusuf, do you think there is a parallel universe? You know, where things are reversed, like there's another me and you out there except I'm a Muslim and you're a Jew. Wait, what if *everything* was in reverse? Imagine a billion Jews surrounding five million Arabs." Sam paused for a moment. And then, a thought. "Do you think that a billion Jews would even *notice* a few million Arabs on this thin slice of land? I bet no Jewish guy would strap on a bomb just to blow up a few Arabs. Yusuf? Are you awake?" Sam listened. Yusuf was asleep.

Potato, thought Sam. Smiling, he closed his eyes.

Yusuf wasn't asleep. He was thinking about what life would be like if Jews surrounded Arabs, and not the other way around.

✦

Sam opened his eyes. It took a second to get his bearings. Propping himself up on his elbows he gazed around. The Dead Sea was directly ahead. It was as calm and still as the desert. To the east, a thin crust of crimson at the rim of the horizon suggested a fine day. It was odd, he thought that he should feel panicky, but he didn't. Maybe it was the place. Sam ran his tongue over his teeth and lips. He could taste salt. His mouth felt like a bale of hay had been parked in it overnight.

It was then that he saw Yusuf. He was on his knees, his forehead and nose touching the sand, his legs curled under him. Sam could hear gentle murmurings. Yusuf was pray-ing. Sam lay back, closed his eyes, and drifted off to sleep.

"Wake up! I got you some water." Yusuf, grinning, held something over Sam's head.

Sam shaded his eyes and looked up at Yusuf. "You look like a bug."

Yusuf touched the rim of the ugly glasses and smiled. "That's what my sister said. Water?" He dangled a paper cup.

"Where did you get it?" Sam reached for the water.

"I got the cup out of the garbage," replied Yusuf. Sam turned up his nose. "There's a hose back there with fresh water. I washed it out! You are a fussy old lady." Yusuf pulled off a shoe and poured out a stream of sand.

"Bug." Sam swigged the water back in two gulps.

"All right, listen, old lady. We have time for a swim. See the sign up by the building? It says that a bus to Jerusalem will be here by 6:00 a.m. I think it's about 5:30." Yusuf looked toward the rising sun, then emptied the other shoe of sand. If he was going to be caught, if he was going to be taken to jail and sent back home without medical care, he would at least be able to say, "I swam in the Dead Sea."

Sam looked up past the beach to broad steps that led to a wooden building. It was light enough to make out signs in Hebrew, Arabic, and English. There was a turnstile in front of the building and beside it a blue awning sheltering white plastic beach chairs. Beyond was an empty parking lot. He scanned the coast and saw their footprints in the sand. They had come over a small sand dune. And then it hit Sam suddenly. Funny how he had not noticed it until now. There was no pain in his leg. He didn't look down. What was there to see? Just a log in a pant leg. He tried moving it. Nothing. He thought of his foot, imagined it moving. Nothing. He closed his eyes and concentrated on wiggling his toes. Nothing. It was dead, it was over, and oddly he felt . . . nothing.

"Did you hear me? We can swim." Yusuf yanked his shirt over his head, undid the top button of his pants, dropped them, and stood in his underwear.

Sam tried to squirm out of his own pants. At first he did his best to move his upper body back and forth and inch the leg out.

"Let me help." Yusuf grabbed the cuffs of the pant legs and pulled. Sam's right leg was too swollen. The material caught.

"Rip it," said Sam.

Yusuf grabbed the material in two fists and yanked. The material tore along the seam. Yusuf held back a gasp. Sam's ankle was the size of a melon, and the skin was pulled so tight it looked like it might split. The foot and ankle were blue, but there were no cuts or open sores.

"Are you in pain?" Yusuf asked. Sam shook his head. "Can you stand?" he asked. Again Sam shook his head. Yusuf pushed the glasses up his nose and peered up and down the beach. "What are those?" Yusuf pointed to a white blur along the shoreline.

"Rescue boards," said Sam.

"Wait here." Yusuf ran toward the boards.

"Wait here? You think I might go dancing . . . cruise over to Jordan to meet the queen?" Sam bellowed after him.

Yusuf returned lugging a long, smooth, white board. "You still okay?" He was trying to sound casual, trying to keep the concern out of his voice.

Sam nodded. "Yeah, I'm okay." He took a deep breath.

"Get on." Yusuf dropped the board beside Sam and tossed the ugly glasses on the pile of clothes. Dragging the offending leg, Sam rolled onto the board. "Hold on," Yusuf cried as he scrambled behind and, with toes and knees burrowing into the sand, pushed. He pushed and pushed until the tip of the board touched the water's edge. Then it skimmed the water and shot out onto the sea like a bullet.

Once he was far enough away from shore, Sam rolled off the board, and in a moment both boys were bobbing around, buoyed by the salty chemicals.

"We can float because of the bromine, magnesium, and iodine," said Yusuf.

"You got that off the Internet, right?"

"Yes."

"You're kind of a geek, aren't you?" Sam swirled his arms across the skin of the water. It felt good, silky and almost luxurious.

"I am a Greek?" Yusuf was confused.

"No, I said a *geek*, not Greek. It's English. It means that you're a nerd." Sam rolled his eyes.

"If nerd means that I am smarter than you, then yes," said Yusuf.

"You are not."

"I am too."

"*I* didn't get hit in the head by a potato."

"I should have let you think I was in an explosion," muttered Yusuf.

"It's too late now." Sam bobbed like a cork as he gazed up at the lightening sky. "What do you think would happen if we just drifted over to Jordan?" he asked.

"Someone would shoot us," replied Yusuf.

"Yeah, someone is always trying to shoot us. That's not normal. The man who lives beside us, Mr. Rosenthal, says that a person can only be normal in normal times. I don't think we live in normal times. I don't think we even live in a normal place." Sam laid his head back and floated.

"How did *you* really get hurt?" asked Yusuf.

"My friend Ari had a new soccer ball. We were passing it back and forth, I missed a pass, ran after it into the street, and got hit by a military truck," Sam said, flatly. He remembered it all now.

"Didn't your mother ever tell you to look both ways before crossing the street?" asked Yusuf.

"Potato," said Sam. Then, after a while, "Ari and I were best friends. He doesn't visit."

"When I am home, my friends do not come to see me either," said Yusuf.

Occasionally they nudged the board to keep it from floating too far away. Rocked by the gentle movement of the water, Sam looked casually toward a shoreline that seemed jumpy in the early light. He squinted, then looked again. His brow furrowed. "Jeez, border patrol!" He was close to screaming.

"Where?" Yusuf swung his arms over the board and tried to focus. It was all a blur.

Sam threw his own arms over the board and narrowed his eyes into slits. The policemen on shore up near the parking lot planted their feet as if rooting themselves in the earth. One had a hand on his hip; the other stood with arms crossed. Sam looked again and again. No guns. Could it be? Was it possible?

"Abba," Sam whispered. The tears in his eyes were sudden. He took a deep breath and lifted his hand. "Abba, Abba!" he cried. "Yusuf, Alina got the text. They're here! They came." His arm was in the air, waving back and forth. But then another thought rushed in as quickly as the first. What if his father was angry?

"Who is it?" No matter how hard Yusuf looked he could see nothing.

"There are two people. The other man—I think it's your father!" said Sam.

"Baba is here too?" Yusuf hoisted himself up and swung one leg over the board. Saltwater got into his eye and stung. He rubbed it while turning around once, twice.

"Listen to me—the text went through. Alina told them that we were here. Wave," cried Sam.

Yusuf looked around. Wave? What wave? There were no waves!

"Your hand. Wave your hand!" Sam, still tense, unsure, and half afraid, watched the shoreline for a reaction.

"Can they see us?" cried Yusuf as he did his best to make sense of the shapes on shore.

"Only if they are in Jordan. You're facing the wrong way."

"Oh!" Yusuf spun around. The board rocked as if in a storm, knocking Sam in the head.

"Watch it. You're a lot blinder than you let on, aren't you?" Sam rubbed his temple.

"What are they doing now?" Yusuf waved his arm faster, like a flag on top of a conquered hill.

"Nothing. Talking, I guess. I never thought I would see such a thing. Should we go in?" Sam hesitated.

Yusuf lowered his hand. It was as if they both had the same thought at the same time. How much trouble were they in?

"What do you think will happen to us?" asked Yusuf.

"I think we'll go back to the hospital," said Sam.

"What I mean is us—Israel, Palestine," said Yusuf. "Are we just going to go on fighting like this forever? Arguing over who's right and who's wrong, like our fathers and our grandfathers and our great-great-a-hundred-great-grand-fathers? Even people who do not live here tell us to fight! Maybe we will be shooting at each other one day. Have you thought of that? Maybe our children and our grandchildren and their children will be trying to kill each other." They stopped flapping in the water and floated. Neither made any effort to paddle closer to shore. Neither had even imagined having children before, let alone children who would carry on shooting and blowing each other up.

"My father says that peace will come when everyone is finally tired of fighting," said Sam.

"I do not think Israelis will ever get tired, not without a miracle, many miracles."

"So, why not? Miracles happen," said Sam.

"*Kol wahad wanasibu*. It means 'to each his fate.' It means that our lives were written in Allah's book before we were born," said Yusuf.

"My aunt's name was Yael."

"She was the one that was killed. I am sorry," said Yusuf.

"Why? You didn't do it. She was really pretty, like Alina. When I was little I thought she could float. She used to dance around the house, her arms waving in the air. I told you, she used to read me stories and tell me jokes."

The sun was up. They were very near the edge of the beach now.

"Knock, knock . . ." said Sam.

"Hello," said Yusuf.

"No, I say, 'Knock, knock.' You say, 'Who's there?'" Sam huffed like a little kid.

"I know. You say, 'Thank you,' and I say, in English, 'You are welcome.'"

"Just say, 'Who's there?' Get it? Okay, let's try it again. Ready?"

"Ready," said Yusuf.

"Knock, knock."

"Come in."

"No! Knock, knock." Sam was getting flustered.

"Enter."

"You're fooling, right?"

"My little sister tells knock-knock jokes. You *still* think that Palestinians know nothing of the world." Yusuf laughed.

"I just don't think of Palestinians as telling jokes."

"We are very funny people," replied Yusuf, straight-faced.

"Yeah, that's the first thing that comes to mind when I think of Palestinians—'Oh, here comes a comedian.'" Sam splashed Yusuf, who immediately returned the favor.

"Want to know the first thing that comes to mind when I think of an Israeli?"

"No."

"What are they doing now?" asked Yusuf.

Sam squinted. The sun was coming up behind the two men. It was getting harder to see. "Still talking, I think."

"Are you on Facebook?" asked Yusuf.

"Yeah," replied Sam.

"Forget knock-knock jokes. Here's one," said Yusuf. "A blind guy on a bus says to the man beside him, 'Do you want to hear an Israeli joke?' The man says, 'Are you kidding? We are in Tel Aviv. I'm an Israeli. That guy over there is an Israeli. The guy in front of you is an Israeli. The two people behind you are Israelis. Are you sure you want to tell that joke?' The blind guy says, 'Not if I have to explain it five times.'" Yusuf was talking fast. They didn't have much time left.

"That's not an Israeli joke, that's a regular joke and you changed the names. You got it off the Internet." Sam chuckled.

"So what?" Yusuf shrugged. "Did you hear about the Israeli who got locked in a grocery store and died of starvation?"

"Fine, did you hear about the Palestinian who brought a knife to a shootout?" said Sam.

"That's old," said Yusuf. They were close to land. Standing in the water up to his waist, Sam put one hand on the board and tried to root his good foot in the sand under the water. The board bobbed and then skimmed across the water.

"Whoaaa!" Sam flailed, his arms slicing the air like pinwheels.

Sam's father leapt up and raced across the beach toward him, Yusuf's father too. The two men were running at top speed, but it was Yusuf who reached across and wrapped his arm around Sam's middle. "I got you."

In the next moment Sam was in Abba's arms. His father lifted him out of the water and staggered to the shore. "It's all right, it's all right," his father whispered. Gently he laid his son on the sand, looked down at Sam's leg, and let out a breath.

"Abba, I need to tell you something. It was my fault. Don't blame Yusuf."

Abba wasn't listening. Already he was standing, his back to Sam, frantically punching numbers into his phone. "We need an ambulance. We will meet you halfway, Route 1 . . . yes, yes." Abba's voice was low and commanding as he gave the dispatcher the information. Once again he was a military officer.

Sam looked over at Yusuf. It was hard to see. Yusuf's father was kneeling in front of his son. His back was to Sam, making it impossible for Sam to tell if he was angry, relieved, or both.

"Abba, please. You have to tell them that it was me. It was all my fault. Don't let anyone get mad at Yusuf for leaving the hospital. He has to have the surgery . . ." Again Sam tried to get his father's attention.

Abba knelt down and touched the bad leg. "Are you in pain?" he asked.

"No." Sam shook his head. He looked up at his father. "Abba, please listen."

"Later. We have to get you both into the car. Put your arms around my neck." Abba kneeled beside Sam. "You both have to get back to the hospital immediately."

EPILOGUE

❖

Six Months Later

I think this is where we're supposed to meet her." Sam looked down at the map, then up at the sign. Owl-like, Yusuf twisted his neck around, up and down, back and forth. He was looking for Alina too, but there was so much else to see. It was sunset and the walls of the Old City, lit by colored lights, glowed golden brown, frosty green, and buttery yellow. He had been in for his last checkup at Hadassah Hospital, so maybe this was the last time he would be in Israel, at least for a long, long time.

The best part of all was that Yusuf could actually *see*. The eye-patch was gone. His fake eye didn't look fake, and besides, he wore glasses now, nice glasses. Alina said that he looked like a law student or a young professor.

Alina was getting better, slowly. She didn't have to stay in the hospital overnight anymore.

"Do you think she's lost?" asked Sam.

"I think maybe you are lost," said Yusuf.

"Well if I'm lost then you're lost too, and so is he." Sam jerked his head back toward the soldier who was supposed to be babysitting them. Every time they turned a corner they had to wait for him to catch up. Sam's father had arranged this outing with the hospital. It had taken a little doing (it had taken a lot of doing) but in the end, Yusuf, in the company of an Israeli soldier, had been given permission to leave the hospital grounds with Sam.

"I'll call her." Sam reached for his phone.

As if on cue, Alina popped out of an alley. Shopping bags dangled from each hand. She wore skinny jeans, a black T-shirt, loopy earrings, and orange running shoes. The wig was gone. A black band covered her ears and a curly mop of golden-brown hair surrounded her face like a fuzzy halo. She was still pale but her smile was huge. The stem cell transplant was working.

"Are you two still arguing? Maybe you both should think of going to university in the United States. You could argue for four years!"

"Be nice. I'm the one with the map." Sam waved the guidebook around.

"It has not helped much so far." Yusuf grinned.

"Hey, I got you to all the holy places you wanted to see."

"We followed the signs!" Yusuf pointed up. He had visited the most holy Muslim sites in the Old City, including the Al-Aqsa Mosque, where Mohammed was transported during the Night Journey from Mecca, and the Dome of the Rock, where the Prophet made his way to heaven to join Allah. He'd prayed at the shrine of the Dome, grateful to be there, and returned with a flushed face and a huge grin. Sam had waited patiently outside. Without special permission, only Muslims could enter their holy places.

"How are you feeling?" Sam asked Alina, the question they were both thinking.

"I'm good. It's likely that a cancer will recur somewhere one day. I might not grow old, but I *will* grow up." She shrugged and smiled. "You know, '*L'Chaim*: to life!'" She did a silly dance.

Neither Sam nor Yusuf felt like dancing.

"Okay, stay grumpy, but no fussing over me, got it? And if you don't want to know, don't ask." Both boys nodded. "So, where's your babysitter?" Alina asked Yusuf.

All three looked around for Yusuf's guard. "He's on his pelly arguing with his girlfriend." Sam motioned to the guard, who was making huge gestures with his free hand as he talked on the phone.

"Okay, what's left to see?" Alina looked at her watch.

"We're done. Let's eat!" said Sam as he waved at the guard.

Over the next few hours the three stuffed themselves with falafel and hummus in the Muslim Quarter, cruised through the Jewish Quarter, and took a wrong turn at the Armenian Quarter before heading up into the Christian Quarter, where church bells were clanging.

It was as if all three were being gently tugged along by an invisible hand. Sometimes they were twitched left, sometimes nudged right, but on they went through a maze of meandering alleys, tunnels, and crooked pathways. Tiny shops embedded in nooks and crannies extended out into the lanes. Every stall was peopled by hawk-faced men dangling their wares: jewelry, clothes, scarves, backpacks, toys, crosses, beads, and religious trinkets of all sorts. Sacks of red, orange, and saffron-colored spices seasoned the air. Silver and gold bangles, colored stones, rugs, T-shirts—the whole world was on display. There was more than history here, more than the three religions. In this place, past and present were one. And maybe the future was here too.

"I would never get bored here," said Yusuf.

Sam leaned on his cane and looked around. Seeing it through Yusuf's eyes, he thought that maybe the place was pretty cool after all.

"How's the leg?" Yusuf asked. They had been walking for a long time.

Sam nodded. He could walk on his fake leg, even run with it, although not very well and not very far, not yet anyway. His new leg, just the part from the calf down, was held on by suction and didn't hurt a bit. It looked pretty good too. He would not need the cane much longer.

"I have a new joke," Sam announced as they set out down David Street. Alina and Yusuf groaned. "Listen. Day after day, an American woman sees a man praying passionately and loudly in front of the Western Wall," said Sam.

"What's it west of?" asked Yusuf.

"I don't know."

"So it could be the Eastern Wall."

"No, it couldn't." Sam, flustered, rolled his eyes.

"Why not?"

"Because I said so, now shut up!"

"You shut up!"

"You two are impossible. You're like two old men." Alina looked from one to the other. "Yusuf, the Western Wall is what remains of an ancient wall that surrounded the Jewish Temple's courtyard. It's where Jews go to pray. They write little messages on paper and stick them in the wall."

"I'm impressed." Sam looked at Alina. Really, he was! He didn't know half that stuff.

"So what's the joke?" Yusuf asked.

"I'll start again."

"No!" both Alina and Yusuf cried.

"Fine. On the last day of the woman's holiday her curiosity gets the better of her and she asks the man, 'Pardon me, you seem to be praying very hard. May I ask, what are you praying for?' He says, 'I pray for peace between the Jews and the Arabs and for our children to grow up in safety and friendship.' So she says, 'Do you think your prayers will work?' The old guy sighs and says, 'It's like talking to a wall.'" Sam grinned.

"Are we going the right way?" asked Yusuf.

"I don't think so," said Alina.

"Wait, that was a great joke!" Sam's voice hit high C.

"It was a joke, not great," said Alina.

"We should go that way," said Yusuf.

"Listen. If you are both quiet I will take you to Jafar's candy store!" said Alina.

Two grinning heads bobbed silently.

Alina shook her head. "You're both six! Come on." She took the lead.

Sam gave Yusuf a friendly push. Yusuf nudged him back.

"Whooah . . ." Sam almost lost his balance.

Yusuf wrapped his arm around Sam's middle. "It's okay, I got you."

If you want to make peace,
you don't talk to your friends.
You talk to your enemies.

—Moshe Dayan (1915–1981),
Chief of Staff of Israel's armed forces,
Minister of Defense and Minister of
Foreign Affairs in Israel's government

If we don't air our grievances,
we'll never get past them.

—Dr. Izzeldin Abuelaish,
Palestinian, and author of *I Shall Not Hate:*
A Gaza Doctor's Journey on the Road to
Peace and Human Dignity

Notes

Hadassah Medical Center

The Hadassah Hospital was nominated for the Nobel Peace Prize in 2005 in acknowledgment of its equal treatment of all patients, regardless of ethnic and religious differences, and efforts to build bridges to peace. Its services are available to all the communities in Palestine. The Hadassah Medical Center organization operates two campuses, with university hospitals at Ein Kerem and Mount Scopus in Jerusalem.

Hamas

Hamas is a Palestinian militant Islamist group that was formed in 1987 to oppose Israel's occupation of the West Bank and Gaza. Its goal is to establish an Islamic state on all the territory historically known as Palestine, including the state of Israel. It is considered a terrorist group by Israel, the United States, and the European Union, but is seen by its supporters as a legitimate fighting force defending Palestinians against Israeli occupation.

Israel

The state of Israel was created in 1948 to be a Jewish homeland by dividing the former territory of Palestine. The Arab population disputed the new state of Israel's jurisdiction over the area. Complicating the conflict is the fact that Jews, Muslims, and Christians all have sites in Israel, many in the Old City of Jerusalem, that they consider holy to their religion. Israelis and Palestinians have been in conflict over the right to live in the area ever since.

Keffiyeh / kufiya
A *keffiyeh* is a traditional Arab headdress or scarf, usually made of cotton. It is typically worn by Arab men and provides protection from the sun and blowing sand.

Kippah (plural *kippot*)
A *kippah*, also known as a *yarmulke*, is a small cap traditionally worn by Jewish men to observe the religious rule that their heads be covered, especially during prayer.

Old City of Jerusalem
The ancient city of Jerusalem, built in 1004 BCE, is a holy place for Jews, Muslims, and Christians alike. The Old City has been home to settlements for thousands of years, but the walls we currently see were built in the early 1500s. Because of the potential for conflict here, the security presence is strong.

Palestinian Authority
The Palestinian Authority (PA) was created in 1994 by the Palestine Liberation Organization and the government of Israel as part of a five-year plan to create a peace accord that would settle the conflict between Israelis and Palestinians. Its primary role today is to provide security and civil government in the West Bank.

Settlements / Settlers
Settlements are Jewish civilian communities—some as large as cities—built on land that Israel captured in the 1967 Six-Day War. These settlements are considered illegal by the International Court of Justice and are considered by many to be an obstacle to the peace process. Settlers view this land (known as Judea and Samaria) as part of the territory promised to them in the Old Testament.

Sidelocks

Sidelocks are curls of hair worn by men and boys in the Orthodox Jewish community to observe the biblical rule that they not cut the hair on the corners of their head.

West Bank and Gaza

The West Bank and Gaza are territories adjacent to Israel that are inhabited predominantly by the Arab/Palestinian population. There are parts of the West Bank under full Palestinian control, where it is illegal for an Israeli to enter; areas in which Palestinians have control over civil matters (e.g., roads and schools) but which are still patrolled by Israeli soldiers; and also an area under full Israeli control, including the highways running to the Jewish settlements. Gaza has not been under the control of the Palestinian Authority since the Hamas coup of 2006.

Acknowledgments

I have always loved writing the acknowledgments. Here is where I freely admit that writing fact-based fiction is truly a collaborative process. But this small book may garner conflicting opinions, and so I list (mostly) first names.

Help came from everywhere: Jerusalem, the West Bank, Canada, and the United States. My thanks to Helen, Margaret and George, Raghida and Amer, Ibrahim and Yamen, Ada, Linda, Kathy, Joan, Elan, Denise, Judy, Sunita, Ann, Donna, and Deborah.

Avi and Michal graciously gave me a place to stay in Jerusalem, and Judith gave me her friendship and advice. My thanks to Samer, who put a roof over my head in the West Bank, Beit Sahour.

No fewer than three doctors checked the medical references in the manuscript: Ron, Jeffery, and Michael.

Hadassah University Medical Center allowed me to tour their facility and answered a flurry of e-mails with grace. Their nomination for the Nobel Peace Prize in 2005 was well deserved.

Barbara Berson edited, and Catherine Marjoribanks dragged me through copyediting. Thanks to Jennifer McClorey and Claudia Kutchukian for proofreading. At Annick, my thanks to Chandra Wohleber, and to Kong Njo for his amazing cover and design.

Dan Lafrance, graphic artist, gave me invaluable suggestions. I used them all!

Fred Schlomka, director of Green Olive Tours, Israel, was my guide in Jerusalem. His organizational skills were amazing. Thank you, Fred.

And to my husband, my model of dignity and grace, David MacLeod.

Postscript

Alina wears a T-shirt that bears the phrase "Life Takes Time," which was coined by Daniel Oliver Couch of Burlington, Ontario, Canada. Alina, a fictional character, and Danny, a very real young man, shared the same rare cancer, hepatosplenic T-cell lymphoma.

In my vision, Alina will beat the cancer, and while she will not return to competitive tennis, she will go on to earn a degree in theater at Yale University. She will also stay in close touch with Sam and Yusuf.

Danny, who lived with grace and courage, was a graduate of Guelph University, Ontario. He died on December 19, 2011, at the age of twenty-five.